PRINCE NARCISSUS
AND OTHER STORIES

ROBERT SCHEFFER (1863-1926) was born the son of a clergyman at Colmar Alsace. He became private secretary to Carmen Sylva Queen of Romania and later, in 1891, went to Paris to devote himself to literature, becoming a contributed to many of the leading magazines, including the *Mercure de France* and *La Revue blanche*. He produced numerous volumes of prose and verse, including *Misère royale* (1893), *Hermeros* (1899), and *Les Frissonnantes* (1905).

SHAWN GARRETT is a freelance editor, critic and short fiction aficionado. He currently co-edits the horror fiction podcast *Pseudopod* and posts weekly columns with *Rue Morgue*, and has a number of other irons in the fire.

SNUGGLY BOOKS

ROBERT SCHEFFER

PRINCE NARCISSUS
AND OTHER STORIES

TRANSLATED BY
SHAWN GARRETT

THIS IS A SNUGGLY BOOK

ISBN: 978-1-64525-014-2

To my mother, Arlene Garrett, whose humor and kindness have been a constant source of strength in my life, and special thanks to my good friend Olivier Nicholas.

—The Translator

Contents

A Note on the Texts

THE contents of the current volume span a period of nine years in the career of Robert Scheffer. The publication information for the various tales is as follows:

"Prince Narcissus" was originally serialized as "Le prince Narcisse: Monographie passionnelle" over two issues of *La Revue blanche*, in September 1896, and then in 1897 was published as an independent volume.

"Anntjö-Mö" was first published in *La Nouvelle Revue*, November-December 1889.

"The Other" was first published as "L'autre" in *L'Initiation*, March 1893.

"The Atonement" was first published as "L'expiation" in *Le Journal*, August 23, 1903.

"The Stranger" was first published as "L'Étrangère" in *Le Journal*, August 1, 1905.

PRINCE NARCISSUS
AND OTHER STORIES

PRINCE NARCISSUS

(*A Study in Passion*)

For J. H. Rosny

I

THOSE who knew Prince Mitrophane Moreano recall his overzealous grace, his overdone elegance, the precious distinction of that curious character who had all the native pride of a great lord but was mannered like a pretty woman in decline. His coquetry could be misunderstood: one could easily be convinced that he only sought to please himself. His manner in offering his hand warned of his indifference to others: his ringed fingers remained tight and stiff, and barely responded to the pressure of handshakes. From his carmine lips, in a soft-toned voice, polite words would fall and he would proffer kind questions to which he hardly expected an answer. Meeting his gaze, one saw an individual who sought less the expression of a thought than the reflection of his own image. The mirrors of a lounge irresistibly attracted him, and he always looked at himself while speaking, correcting with care an unfortunate fold of his face, assuring the symmetry of his coiffure with a pretty gesture, while his mouth flashed a smile as white as his wig, though in some places tarnished by small, delicate and discolored teeth. He worried over the harmony of his tie and clothing and had the affectations of pinning his hair, filling his buttonhole and holding his gloves. His stature was below average, so he wore false, pointed heels which clacked across waxed floors and gave him a jerky step. Yet he praised himself for the correctness of his movements and the perfection of his attitudes, and he profited vastly from his seductive assets.

If, by his singularities, he provoked attention, he also attracted sympathy that arose through the sweetness of his eyes in his charmingly drawn face, the pleasant timbre of his voice, and also by an expressive melancholy which refined, at certain moments, his regular features. A slight lisp did not impede his language, which was a little hesitant but pure, and his occasional Oriental turn-of-phrase recalled his country of origin.

Of his antecedents little was known. We recounted small episodes of his life, whether true or false, as was customary. No doubt he was rich, and the name he bore was illustrious in Romania. He had his official residence in Paris, which was more cosmopolitan than Wallachia, and made extended stays in the various capitals of Europe. For years he had not revisited his homeland. Some people maintained that he was banished after daring to lay claim to his ancestor's throne, while others gossiped that he had exiled himself spontaneously following a scandalous, unspecified adventure. Both versions may have deserved some credit. Not that Prince Moreano's legitimacy in Bucharest was invalid but he himself, convinced of his right to rule, was mortified at the idea of being the subject of a foreign sovereign. And it was true that having dispelled most of his patrimony, and considered poorly by his compatriots, he seemed resigned to live in the West.

Besides, he was often seen with his cousin, Héloïse Caréna, and it was no secret that this princess only admitted the best people into her salons. In fact, only academicians, renowned artists, nobles and notorious personalities were received by this exquisite *Parisienne du Danube* who deigned to be a pianist (and, when at the piano, no one could forget that she was a great lady). When she presented him, with an easy smile and more than usual generosity, it was as "My cousin, Prince Mitrophane Moreano." Her smile and over-pronunciation indicated that she was proud of this relative's sonorous name, and this was enough to classify him among characters of importance. He was exclusively seen in this world, never receiving anyone, and the mystery of his life was impenetrable. Skeptics, who allow themselves to interfere in the affairs of others, said that there was no real mystery and that the prince lived a decent and boring life in his closed apartments. Nevertheless, he *was* known for two fancies: buying paintings—always portraits—and purchasing high-priced mirrors. Since he did not parade his acquisitions for worldly collectors, this clandestine taste for these expensive objects aroused curiosity. Why did he pay so dearly for often mediocre paintings, and what did he do with the mirrors, as he was ascribed no mistress? It was decided that he must do nothing more than contemplate them, and so by his special circle he was referred to as "Prince Narcissus."

Nobody then knew just how well this sobriquet suited him.

II

WHEN he was young, he had a passion for contemplating himself in the pure reflection of mirrors. Idolizing his image, he drew as close as possible to the glass and pressed his lips against it, seeming to seek the fictional kiss of himself, while his gaze plunged drunkenly into the azure abyss of his own eyes. His mother, who had a boundless admiration for the child, never tired of telling him that he was handsome and insisted in asking her friends "Is my son not beautiful?" thus excessively developing the child's already remarkable selfishness.

To a certain extent, the nature of the mother explains the character of the son. Immediately after her marriage she was prone to fits of hysterical madness, which forced her to be closely watched, and yet she one day escaped into the street, naked and obscene. Some joked about it, but doubts persisted as to the origin of the child who came into the world less than a year after the mad flight of this young woman and a few months after the death of her husband, the prince. The father was sought among the many servants of the house and it was generally believed that he was found in a young and handsome Gypsy whom the princess, now cured or nearly so, treated with benevolence. For a Vlach, the term "son of a Gypsy" constituted a notable insult and it would disqualify the child if *Romany* blood was attributed to him. But the mother was of such an aristocratic line that a child born of her flesh was, nevertheless, authentically noble.

In her frenzy of love for the child, she pampered him and obeyed his most fantastic wishes. In the caresses she lavished on him, there was something unfulfilled and bestial, and his imperturbable calm in receiving them was disconcerting. In response to her demonstrations, he would pronounce with an authoritarian gesture: "I want this, I want that," and his caprice was fulfilled. What he asked for were jewels, fine soft fabrics, silk or velvet, lace, and early on he developed a taste for perfumes. Putting on the new, desired outfit, he drew his brown and lustrous mass of hair back against his temples with long, sickly fingers and, perched before a high mirror, smiled to himself in complacency and sadness. He had regular and charming features. His teeth sparkled and his fresh, pink complexion was that of a happy young woman. The blue shadows under his eyes gracefully indicated his frail childhood and, later, a troubled adolescence plagued by a delicate but voluptuous constitution.

By then, the displays of maternal love were less lively and frequent, the handsome Gypsy Dinic having disappeared from the house and the princess having turned her tenderness towards a second husband. The child, who had grown up without much instruction, was entrusted to the care of a tutor. The latter, who had previously been a professor for an aged, crazed, humanitarian *boyar*, was scarcely inclined to favorably modify the tendencies of his ward.

This tutor, a provencial adventurer, had started on a long journey that ended with him stranded in Bucharest, where hospitality was easy and wide, especially back then. He pretended to have been charged with some mysterious political mission, and had enough interpersonal skills to be believed. He also confided, under the seal of secrecy, that he was a Rosicrucian, and an expert in the occult sciences. He had the semblance of sincerity, even when his actions were shady. Perhaps, in special circumstances, he may have actually served as a secret agent in the Danubian principalities and his easy access to certain influential characters tended to make him believable. When he spoke of conspiracies he was serious, if inconsistent, and in all of his speech he was both affirmative and uncertain, his gaze piercing and unstable. Women were fond of him because, far better than the old Gypsies, he read the future in their palms and his pronouncements of good or bad adventures were made in gallant French.

Therefore, this ambiguous stranger was installed in a wing of the Moreano Palace and took charge of the education of the young Mitrophane.

On a hillock at the left edge of the narrow, shallow Dimbovitza was the vast and gloomy locale of the Moreano palace. A crowd of servants flocked there, and yet still it looked desolate in the solitude. The frequent visitors and elegant crews at the front door did not animate it. In the hot summer sun, it dozed in the frail foliage of the acacias and under the dazzling snow of winter its facade rose against the bright blue of the sky, bleak and black. The sleds, white or scarlet covers flapping against the rumps of horses as they caught the wind like proud sails, hurriedly crossed the bumpy street without failing to ring their bells which sounded against the high, gloomy, closed windows of the noisy apartments. There are houses that live their own funerary life, absorbed in the contemplation of the past or future misfortunes they conceal. The Moreano palace seemed predestined to episodes of love and blood. It was one of the oldest dwellings in Bucharest, where most buildings are modern, and there was talk of the dramas that had happened there, but this was only legend. By then only boredom was the undisputed master, and the cracks in the walls announced the decadence of both the house and the strong race that had built it.

Mitrophane loved this house of sorrow. He felt, perhaps with some confusion, that the enclosure was charmed and that it had sheltered his rare flower from the touch and gaze of the vulgar.

The tutor heard those stammering thoughts, cleared and clarified them, and then approved them. Himself, he liked the comfortable place and, with the princess and her recent husband having lost interest in the child, he was left to his own devices. He wished to enjoy his happiness as long as possible through this serendipity. Besides, he cherished his pupil and in turn the pupil, who was indifferent and polite to all, had embraces for him alone.

As a matter of fact, the young boy was not constrained to a regular education and all rigor of discipline was spared him. The adroit Provencal mystic was careful not to tire him with austere and detailed lessons. He taught the prince, at his will and on his improvised schedule, a little history and geography, introduced him to Latin and, with difficulty, inculcated the science of numbers, all while never failing to flatter the boys' pride by extolling his ancestors' prowess, both maternal and paternal. Also, as he grew, the tutor awakened especially the prince's imagination through symbolic tales, wherein he elucidated, in his own way, the famous dictum: "Know thyself."

Whether these esoteric studies were fraudulent or true, the Professor had recognized in Mitrophane a privileged being, an elect of an occult order. In the prince's hand he had deciphered the signs of a singular destiny and when the tarot was consulted it did not contradict these predictions, although it spoke more obscurely. The precocious love that the little one held for himself and his attraction to mirrors (where no doubt he basked in the revealing astral light reflected by the splendor of his "future self") confirmed to the Professor that the last Moreano was fated for a superior and important mission. The signs in his hand and the algebra of the tarot (the former precise in its figuration, the latter infallible in its formulas) presented dual faces of truth to disappointed interpreters. But he loved the haughty restraint of the wonderfully pretty child just as fervently, but perhaps with less effusion, than the princess. Perhaps the Rosicrucian himself had cultivated in his pupil this passion for reflections, and had voiced these augural fancies simply to curry favor. He showered the prince with compliments, just like the boy's mother had, and the large azure eyes of

Mitrophane seduced him as though he tottered on the edge of an abyss full of rare, blooming flowers.

On entering puberty, Mitrophane was gripped by a sudden lassitude which required short and immediate naps, during which he uttered fragmentary sentences which, taken in isolation, were strange and sometimes of an abrupt beauty.

The clairvoyant master concluded that his subject had miraculous lucidity and resolved to test it. He took the opportunity during one of these unexpected and irresistible sleeps to question the prince.

At the first questions, the answers were soft and undecided. Mitrophane awoke upon speaking and refused to go back to sleep.

The Rosicrucian was not discouraged. He renewed his experiments, preparing them with talks on magic, on the manifestations of the soul, on the gift of second sight. When the young man was asleep, he made strange signs over him and clasped his hand with more ardor than perhaps was necessary to communicate his will. It seemed that he had succeeded in his project, for Mitrophane, in these prolonged slumbers, spoke with satisfactory cohesion and described surprising visions. Returning to himself from the preceding dream, his face held a reflection of light, his thoughts continued to travel through distant and nebulous regions, and he approached the clarifying mirror to consider himself. The image of his positive being was hidden from his sight, and hovering in a wide and radiant space was a transparent form of sweet and colorful contours. He sent fervent kisses towards it and without haste the ghost dissolved, flowed like limpid water, and then reformed as his own firm and opaque body. Mitrophane sighed and, passing his hand over his forehead, turned away.

One evening in early spring, after a long walk in the luminous and deserted Romanian countryside, the young man had a slight, feverish chill. He went to bed and, as soon as he was asleep, he began to speak. He stammered: "I am the Virgin, the Prostitute—I am the Prostitute, the Virgin," and indulging in this antithesis, repeated it to satiety. And then, a brief voice concluded: "I am Love." And as the amazed tutor touched his shoulder and asked "Who do you say you are?" he reiterated "I am Love," with an expression upon his face both sublime and prodigious.

The prince rose slowly, climbed down from his bed, opened his eyelids (whose long black lashes still lent them a dreamy look of mystery) and with fixed, wide and shining eyes, his arms above his inspired head and his pink fingers stretched towards the suspended lamp, he advanced to the center of the room, then stopped.

"Listen!" he said.

And, with something like the broken rhythm and inharmonious but bewitching melody of prestigious Gypsies, he intoned a strange song, unmoving and low at first until he raised his voice and gestured. With a sudden movement he undid his shirt and threw it like a white bird across the room, the marble of his young flesh shining.

The hymn he improvised was to his own glory, broken by the chorus of "I am the Virgin, the Prostitute" which he chanted in a strange and monotonous voice.

The Rosicrucian, meanwhile, simply listened and watched.

Facing the mirror and sobbing, the ephebe made as if to embrace his reflection. His frail body vainly pressed against the cold crystal, and he fiercely applied his lips, tarnishing the glass with mist in which his own image disappeared. Then he drew back, uttering a groan and his hands beat the air. As he was about to fall, his professorial friend received him in his arms and carried him to his bed, where by gentle caresses and words he was appeased.

As a result of this curious crisis of somnambulism and adolescence, Mitrophane was deemed ill enough that the doctors thought it expedient to send him to a foreign country where the air would be healthier, to complete his education.

Mitrophane's eyes filled with tears when his tutor took leave of him, as he held some affection for this great friend. As it turned out, he would never see him again. The Rosicrucian, having undertaken the initiation of a venerable and opulent widow into magic, was chased down by a rival and forced into a lawful duel. He was brought down by a mere shot piercing his temple, despite all of his evil spells, incantations, talismans and other symbols of the cabalistic panoply.

Mitrophane, the narcissistic child, could not have met a more pernicious guide in his early years than this whimsical tutor, an equivocal knight of love and a wizard of contraband. True, his vehement mother had transmitted to him the germ of passionate troubles and his Eastern ancestry predisposed him to mystic visions and exaltations, but through guilty practices and superficial, dangerous teachings the semi-Rosicrucian had led Mitrophane to the wavering threshold of the supernatural world, cultivating in him that blossom of self-love through ceaselessly and unreservedly admiring the prince.

At an early age, adorned with ornaments, perhaps this modern Narcissus sought to recognize in the depths of his own eyes the beauty of his soul, but instead he now relented more and more to satisfaction with his own body, taking vanity from each of his assets. His time in a Swiss boarding school, where he was treated as a great exotic lord, did not cure him of himself. Comrades, seduced by his feminine grace, were eager for his company and he was benevolent to them, accustomed as he was to such homage. And yet he never fully dropped the reserve which sealed him off, as if encased in a magic circle. Therefore some were more fond of him than reason dictated while others did not dare make fun of him, and the attention shown him confirmed the desire that he inspired. Loving no one, he needed to be loved, in order to love himself better.

A few years passed and, now a man, he returned to his native land, free in his actions.

In the meantime, his mother had divorced. Having founded a refuge for noble and poor widows, she enjoyed general esteem and the home she had built near the Moreano refuge was a place of celebration. There were many games, and entertainments of every kind abounded there. No one was scandalized that this esteemed lady would provide for the needs of a young orphan who was as poor and noble as the meritorious widows and, moreover, who had strong portions of male beauty.

The prince found himself living alone in his palace. The center of the city having moved, he was even more isolated than before, surrounded by grounds rendered bare from recent demolitions. What, eventually, would be a pleasant walk, at that time consisted mostly of piles of rubble wreathed in febrile miasmas.

He made himself comfortable in the wing that he had formerly occupied, with his tutor, as a child, and left the rest of the abandoned palace empty. Living apart in this taciturn residence suited him. For a long summer he led a contemplative existence there, closed to joy. His nonchalance adapted easily to the heat which overwhelmed the Romanian countryside in that season.

He loved to see the sun gleaming and the white houses stretching to infinity over the pale curtains of greenery. Above the low roofs, at a slight incline, emerged the crowd of bulbous blue and green church towers, whose broad, golden terminal crosses barbed the clear azure sky. And not very far away, on the mound opposite, dozed the massive metropolitan church whose big bell sounded out for feast days in waves of grave and religious clamor. Beyond the town, past the wooded heights where the old convent (now the melancholy royal residence of Cotroceni) aligned its white quadrilateral, even beyond the city itself lay the red plain. And there extended the dull ribbon of the river, in whose shallow water glittered the incessant, robust, nude bathers. Voluptuousness was latent in the motionless air and, especially at night, the disintegrating pleasure and ineffable beauty of the transparent sky was splendid. On the narrow terrace of his roof, Mitrophane lay on cushions, stretching and dreaming under the stars. His virility slumbered as well and no carnal desire obsessed him, although that sister of love, intense and exquisite sadness, which is more dangerous by far, visited him. Conquered by the lascivious charm of the warm atmosphere, he was defenseless and became subject to the deceptive embrace of his unconscious. Into the enormous and confounding mirror of the sky, where many marvelous figures regularly appear, he projected his own face and admired himself for so long that he grew drowsy. Then, lazily, he would sample some sherbet while smoking half a cigarette of blond tobacco mixed with fragrant *kief,* and wrap himself in the soft cloak of dreams. He remembered the teachings of the Rosicrucian and the supernatural manifestations that had followed them. Those glimpses of mystery charmed him and under the caress of vague and troubling thoughts his indecisive soul languished. Had he not pronounced: "I am the Virgin, the Prostitute, I am Love!"? And, certainly, he was all of that, and loved himself . . . ah, but to what end? He shivered with pleasure to feel the elegant outline of his frail body under the light fabric of his clothes. He knew that, under the night sky full of stars, his weary smile was filled with sweetness. He knew the appeal of his lips and his eyes, kissed by the rays of those exhilarated stars, was irresistible. And what a torment, what delicious and refined torture, to be the proper object of his own worship: desired by all, to desire only oneself and yet to oneself be unobtainable forever . . . "If there was a being who is perfect like me . . . could he exist somewhere? And if this being now sat near me, would I be happy?" he wondered. Like the famed hermaphrodite turning his face from the sky, he plunged softly into the loose silk of the cushions and folded his arms under his chest, in order to meditate better on the enigma that he himself represented. He was the sum—or so he had been told—of his race, and in himself he loved all those who had preceded him. This mirage of anterior epochs rich beyond measure, saturated with tears and splendid with the love of those who were also him, flattered his present indolence. He conceived that action had ebbed away in these successive hands and now, engendered by dreams, it returned again, dispersing itself through the dream. And he, Mitrophane, was the figure of death and transition who, in scrutinizing his own gaze, regarded inertly the tumultuous glory of the past and the mobile mists of the future.

He went downstairs to his apartments, and into a room full of mirrors.

Here, after stern contemplations, a sudden terror fell upon him, but a terror which was also a supreme pleasure. He *knew* that behind him, repeating his every movement, a hideous being watched him. He *wanted* to see it. Against a bright background of light its gray silhouette stood out. Then, stifling a cry, he *closed his eyes* and remained motionless, frightened, blind, standing before the mirror where his image, his lamentable image, stood blind, frightened, motionless. And when he opened his eyes, the image reflected in his over-excited retina was surrounded by a thin halo, pink with blood and transparent in the candlelight. However, the gray silhouette had dissipated.

"The master is a little crazy," the servants gossiped. But as he was also indulgent, they showed him kindness.

His mother, absorbed by her refuge of noble widows, her gallant lifestyle and her needy orphan, had no time to worry about her son. In truth, it was positively painful for her to hear his name, as he brought to mind an unfortunate episode of her youth. It was also unfortunate that he was the same age as her current, vigorous protégé. Moreover, while in possession of the small but certainly sufficient property of the Moreanos, he had no claim to maternal property, which the dowager intended to dispose of during her lifetime as she pleased. Having completed a holiday in the country, at the foot of the Carpathians, she was visited by Prince Mitrophane as soon as she returned to Bucharest. As there was company with her, she treated him like a foreigner of distinction. Not long after, returning his politeness, she visited him for a brief consultation. The dowager declared the young prince's lifestyle absurd, and did not hesitate to tell him that she found his ways ridiculous. He shook his head and, in a tone of exquisite courtesy, replied:

"You do not understand anything, madame."

"What do you mean, I don't understand? Am I not your mother?"

"Is all this really necessary, madame?"

Suffocated by his impertinence, the dowager had no answer. She went out, slamming the doors behind her. In the opinion of her son, the tall lady had rough manners. He also reflected that his mother usually showed him indifference and that, in order to criticize him, she wrongly took advantage of a quality which she did not boast to the public about at all.

Moreover, proud in his loneliness, it was convenient for him to break the bonds which blind nature establishes between parents and children.

As a result, their relationship was limited to this singular exchange of visits.

The enmity between the mother and son, for a time, was the gossip of Bucharest. But while the lady, in her refuge, ranted about her offspring whom she only referred to by his title, *Prince Moreano*, the latter was silent about her. He had supporters, among whom was his ex-father-in-law, who cared little for him but who had his own reasons for feeling even less affection for the dowager. The aggressive speeches she held against her child scandalized the city. The most charitable supposed that she held his being itself as a remorse. Others insinuated that her gallant orphan dictated her eloquence.

So well known was her anger that Prince Mitrophane, out of boredom, set to work on an innocent revenge. He decided one day that he would open his own salon to receive his mother's guests, and splendidly restored it for the occasion. It was an eccentricity that pleased many and which was widely talked about. Out of curiosity, they came in droves, all familiars of the ex-Princess Moreano, to see this young original who treated his guests so lavishly. And it was said that she had a mental breakdown from the misery she felt that her abandonment would profit her son.

And so, Prince Mitrophane nonchalantly welcomed his guests. After taking the proffered hands of the most notable, and watching over the good order of the feast, he retired to his apartments. Bestowing to the crowd the illuminated rooms, the rich buffet and all the joy that would suit them, he kept for himself his sealed chamber, his pure mirrors, his contemplative and solitary pride.

In fact, he cleverly understood that with his name and at his age he couldn't afford to be ignored by escaping from everyone's sight. And, perhaps glimpsing the miseries of the future, he tried to fight against his own inclinations. In the winter that followed he mingled somewhat with public life, showing himself at the "Chaussée" which, a boring and sad avenue, was the rendezvous of the elegant world. It was also said that he had one or two flirtations. But this kind of life, which he was weary of even before he tasted it, grew odious to him as soon as he forced himself to indulge in it. Judging that it wasn't worth the time, he hastened to put an end to the affair and dismissed his official dolly, not without having paid handsomely for her services. Annoyed with being dropped, she gossiped that the situation had been a profitable bore, making anecdotal and derogatory remarks about her ex-"friend."

She stated decisively that Prince Mitrophane had not inherited the faculties of love possessed by his mother, and that he was of dissolute morals. This was expressed in good society euphemistically, which still did not employ the convenient word of "neurosis" to characterize the habits of those who differ from the general public.

Some details brought a smile to the crowd's lips.

It was learned that Prince Moreano chose blushes, powders, and cosmetics to delight his complexion, and that in order to brighten the shade of his hair, which was dark brown, he applied the use of extraordinary mixtures. He was an expert in the art of embellishing and lengthening his eyebrows, and he knew how to communicate a soft and sustained glow to his charming eyes. His baths were an involved preparation, suave and comforting. Delicate massages softened his thin frame. He paraded before his mirrors with and without a suit, and his bathrobes of transparent linen or soft surah, were often disconcerting. He wore rich dressing-gowns, trimmed with precious furs or exorbitant lace, and fitted with a long train, like a women's. With his brilliantined hair, painted face, and white, bejeweled hands, he seemed less man than girl.

Such were the stories of the courtesan, perhaps truthful and undoubtedly rancorous. For her position had been good and, in spite of his genderless appearance, the prince was liked by women. She narrated more such tales, but to relate them would be useless, as they were not proven and modesty would be offended.

While not very curious about the tales of which he was the subject, Prince Mitrophane could not close his ears entirely to certain gossip. And to confound the vulgar, he planned a dinner and invited some considerable personages. To their surprise, he received them in a long dressing gown and though the house was sufficiently heated, as it was winter, he made them sit around a glowing blaze in the fireplace. He himself occupied the least favorable place, and ostentatiously gathered at his feet the ample train of his garment. After a few minutes of conversation, he left his guests, but soon reappeared, this time in his usual costume. Not without some irony, he apologized for having delayed the hour of the meal by his change of outfit. "But," he explained to them, "I suppose you would be happy to know why I wear long dresses at home. You see, I am chilly and, when sitting or lying down, a train curled around my feet guarantees that they will be warm, as you have seen for yourself. Gentlemen, you will, in favor of my motive, pardon my earlier display." This demonstration astounded his friends, but a table loaded with exquisite food and adorned in perfect taste helped them accept it.

Still, people did not fail to gloat over Prince Moreano. His affair having collapsed, it was spread that the dinner was instigated through guilty generosity. Nothing was specified and every rumor was affirmed. The prince was not mortified by this chatter but, nevertheless, resolved to leave a city where such hostility was shown to him.

Then, the Russo-Turkish war broke out, from which Romania picked laurels, gained independence, and proclaimed a royal crown.

Prince Mitrophane exhibited some bravery, and carried his habits of elegance to the military camp. Naturally indifferent to danger, he was careful that nothing of his attitudinal grace was disturbed, and so he worried far more over his dapper uniform and perfect smile than over mere shells and bullets. Others were grateful for this martial respite, but he got into trouble with a superior officer who treated him without consideration.

Regrettable incidents resulted and, when the war was over, the prince was not included in the role of rewards. Some were astonished, but the well-informed people confided that the War Ministry contained a distressing record of the ex-officer's morality. Nothing was proven and yet nothing was considered more true.

It was then, on the pretext of his removal from the consolidated dynasty, that a half-ruined Prince Moreano sold his ancestral home and moved abroad.

III

A T that time, peculiarities were accentuated in him while his standing deteriorated.

First, early wrinkles brushed his forehead with their light network, then the corners of his mouth, then his temples and finally his neck, whose slender length seemed to him to have the white, undulating look of swimming swans. Noting this wear on his person in the irreproachable Venetian glass, enclosed in a curiously worked oval frame of pewter, was a sorrow to him, the first heartfelt sorrow he had ever experienced. He accused his favorite mirror of betraying him. And yet he paired his wager against age with a more meticulous search, striving to establish the perfect harmony of garment and face, correcting his weaknesses by subtle brush strokes and deft transpositions of hair. Thanks to this happy combination in his physiognomy, he thus kept at a distance the appearance of a small, withered ephebe.

He isolated himself strictly in his home, so that his image in the glass was not tarnished by the reflection of foreign presences. And if he appeared at his cousin Caréna's little salon, it was because its dimensions seemed adequate and the straw-colored curtains harmonized exactly with the iris of his eyes, his complexion, and the immutabe brown shade of his hair.

In addition, her small verdi mirror pleased him. It had an ivory border encrusted with a fine algae of silver, and sat on a Florentine cabinet.

Taken with an indefinable anxiety, he sought to flee himself. Suddenly, without any pretext of a motive, he would travel. Of the countries visited he had few precise memories, except that cities situated at the water's edge moved his imagination better than others, and he spoke unceasingly of their grace.

But the meaning of these trips remained mysterious.

Apart from sovereign personages in small capitals whom he solicited an audience with out of vanity, he did not take the time to become acquainted with anyone, and the new landscapes seemed indifferent to him. It seemed unreasonable that he should leave his comfortable and secure home, since manifestations of art impressed him only slightly and since it did not seem that in distant countries he pursued any special pleasures.

But, at first, it was not exactly assured that while abroad he did not inquire of particular distractions. Some (those idle, international spies) claimed to have recognized him, notwithstanding his disguises, and observed him on several occasions at the most opposite edges of Europe, and supposedly in dubious company.

On returning from his sudden wanderings, he appeared tired, perplexed, and aged. His usual smile bloomed painfully on his lips, and he needed patience and much ingenuity to restore his face to the enviable freshness of a woman's.

Others may treat their pained virility by means of heroic labors or dangerous sports, but he passed his delicate sorrows on to the pumice stone.

A concern for the future had begun to haunt him.

Up until then, and as long as he felt desirable, he was proud of his own passionate anomaly. But now that time was rushing to crush his beauty, he felt himself frightened of feeling dead to himself.

Had the reckless Rosicrucian been mistaken in his prediction of extraordinary destinies? And if being the sole object of one's own worship was not the supreme happiness, was punishment surely not spared to those who delight in the coupled life, for they will see the flesh which reflects their love undergo the slow, irresistible cessation of life? And while vulgar humanity found consolation in reenergizing itself with new passions, where could *he* look? Could he only perish miserably, with no help from anyone who could sympathize with his incurable pain? With no sweeter memories during the final agony than time's juvenile image that he had idolized so much?

Meditating on this he was terrified by the emptiness of his heart and, incapable of exerting the least effort to fill it, he veiled this abyss by evoking vague and puerile ambitions. Projecting the fortune and glory of his birth, in these easy dreams he was a king, bedecked with insignia from his own drawings, offering in spirit his diademed person to the eyes of a seduced crowd. Scenes of his childhood rose up perversely in his memory. Intoxicated by his fictitious sovereignty, he still had not forgotten that he was the Virgin and the Prostitute, and above both, that he was also Love itself.

Then, ensconced in his mirrored circle, surrounded by numerous portraits all of which resembled him in some way, he played strange comedies for himself.

Exalted by his imaginary grandeur, he flashed smiles and greetings that were reflected back by the symmetrical and infinite crowds of himself. This animated him, and he was compelled to speak. He preached his own merits, boasting of his undeniable virginity. But his own voice stunned him and, while initially sober, his gestures became more lively and more grand. Behold, those around him were moving about, reaching with hands of lust, calling to him with their mouths and eyes, drawing him into invincible arms. Suddenly a flood of passion overwhelmed him, he wished to give himself up to this delirious multitude and, energetically denying the chastity he had just proclaimed, Mitrophane shouted: "But no, I am the prostitute, and so come to me all who want to be loved, for I, 'Love,' am here!"

A vertigo seized him. The reflected beings whirled madly and dragged him into their delirious dance.

The portraits, hung on walls or placed on easels, judged his defeat with severity. And the more he surrendered himself to the imperious embrace of his infinite reflections, the more he sensed weighing upon him the mute reprobation of those immobile characters, clothed in the fragmenting forms of his young and most beautiful years.

With the voluptuous suffering that followed such an excessive nervous expenditure, there came appeasement, and shame fell upon him then. He shed tears before the painted images, kneeling before the reminder of what he had once been, asking pardon for his profanation of himself. In adoration, he lit incense and, if taken with sudden attacks of rage, he lacerated the pictures.

During his trips, and when his mania was increased, he especially purchased portraits as well as mirrors, claiming the latter renewed the outline of his own face through the mystery of foreign skies found within their aged frames. In the former he perceived some of his own constituent features, indelibly fixed in the past. Through the rapid play of reflections he united them all into a standard image conjured by himself, and he admired the creative powers that over time and throughout history had created sketches of what he himself would eventually become, the unique and perfect copy.

Perfect? But he had only been so for a moment, and now that moment had passed and would never again reappear!

A hatred of fate, which rejoices in alternating joy and pain, ugliness and beauty, swelled his heart to bursting. In need of revenge, he rushed at the fictions whose convergent glances were his own (along with pitiless destiny's) and in which he—the child—thought to destroy himself!

The vanity of his efforts exhausted him. For comfort, he desired to view and, even taste, blood. But not daring to draw the red life he coveted from his own veins, he rolled on the ground, gasping, and bit his own flesh, without hurting himself terribly. Then, on the thick carpet, surrounded by descending blue vapors of sweet and perfumed incense, he would suddenly fall into a brief sleep during which, for what felt like centuries, he experienced visions of a singular and melancholy sweetness.

Certainly, those who later met him in the street, precious and perfumed, would hardly have imagined the curious delirium to which this exquisite gentleman had been subject. And if Princess Caréna had been warned, she might have refused him entrance to her salon, in spite of his illustrious lineage (whose kin had verified his personal and uncertain title). And so, she might have been spared some problems.

The disorder of his thoughts reverberated into his affairs, and so Prince Moreano, the great purchaser of mirrors and paintings at any cost, the great traveler to bizarre Cytherian countries, neglected certain positive details by which life, otherwise floating and vaporous, takes shape and becomes consistent. Not liking money, he had spent without scruple and now knew financial embarrassment, as happens to the noblest lords. When such pecuniary necessity arose, he did not hesitate to sign the most disadvantageous promissory notes in exchange for good, beautiful gold.

Thus, in a few years, he was stripped almost entirely of the remainder of his fortune. And while it was a wonder for him to become poor, it was not as sad as one might think.

IV

IN fact, he was indifferent to wealth.

He did not take advantage of the Parisian life. If, after his Bucharest errors, he had settled in Paris rather than elsewhere it was by unconscious imitation of most of the internationally ruined and idle, not through any well-defined taste. Thus, filled with self-interest, he remained a stranger to the distractions of the big city and, as it seemed like the right thing to do, refrained from establishing many relationships. His gold he had spread carelessly, or through vanity, and not to satisfy urgent and expensive fantasies but instead on the canvases and mirrors and perhaps the occasionally rare and special exception.

Now that he had to order his lifestyle according to the modest pension that his mother administered, he resolved to change his residence.

During his various migrations, one city had shown its favor: Venice.

Leaning over her lagoons, as over some vast and propitious mirror, it seemed the city enjoyed itself no less than he did in his own contemplation.

"No doubt," he expounded, in the style of the deceased Rosicrucian. "No doubt this city is in love with itself. For cities do not grow at random in a specific place, like plants, but a will presides over their birth. They are a rich and complex body animated by a spirit. They are born, develop, catch diseases, and die. Their appearance conforms to the spirit that created them and it chooses carefully the site they occupy, so that it is in perfect harmony with itself.

"But the soul of Venice is as peculiar as the city it inhabits. She is of a unique beauty, she has realized her dream in precious and solid architecture and according to rhythms unknown to others, who came before her.

"She wanted to flourish in a quiet basin, nearby but safe from the indiscreet crowd of waves, that she might sit and admire herself there. And my own self, born mobile, captures and immobilizes my vision of humanity in the false water of mirrors, and I am satisfied with my own appearance.

"The sumptuous silence of Venice agrees with me.

"Within the narrow border of her canals I will be more unpredictable to myself, like those solitary fig trees which, from a quay between two pink palaces, grow towards the water which reflects their stray blossoms."

Having identified, not without some affectation of his own sensations, with the soul of the nonchalant city, he resolved to stay there.

And in staying there he was not disappointed.

It was the right place for his mood.

Having taken a cheap apartment on one of the most out-of-the-way canals, opening on Murano, he rather opulently furnished some rooms with the fragments of his luxury, and left the rest abandoned.

The ceilings were low and curved. There were traces of gilding on the door frames, and peeling paint on the panels. The warped floor was imbedded with mosaics disappearing under the woolen heraldic designs of deep carpets. On the irregular walls there were brocades which gleamed with metal and heroic bundles of arms, a reminder of the valiant Moreano line. Comfortable seats were scattered about the place, wherever they fit best. A divan of sufficient width occupied the back of an alcove, and was surmounted by a perfect mirror. It illuminated, as if from a lunar reflection, the shadowy recess.

A green light from below rose into the windows, which framed in their marble columns the white arch of a bridge and the exquisite and dilapidated facade of a patrician abode. The sun's rays, blocked by an elbow of the canal, only discreetly crept into the rooms, and so mystery remained there. Prince Mitrophane, in such dim daylight, did not suffer from seeing much that affirmed the aging of his person.

V

IT would be superfluous to narrate the monotonous existence that he led from then on. Some details will establish the transition to the tragic event that concluded his stay.

One of his first actions, faithful to princely tradition, was to go call on the Royal Highness who lived in Procuratie Nuove, but his visit having not been reciprocated, he felt offended and renounced all worldly habits.

He knew how to absent himself completely from the joyful and colorful life of Venice. He was not seen at the afternoon music on the Piazza, nor in the cafes along the galleries, nor during the feast days when the gondolas illuminated the Grand Canal. The commercial bustle of certain alleys, such as the Merceria, was odious to him. In his opinion the loquacity of the *barcaroli* and *facchini* dishonored the noble Riva degli Schiavoni, so he avoided passing through there except in the depths of night or in the burning, drowsy noontime. As for the glass factories, he ignored them, and he was rarely seen at the Academy.

But, far from the city, he was fond of prolonged wanderings between sky and water, so that in the illusory depths of the flat lagoons he could contemplate the singular landscape of the high clouds and those inverted houses and campaniles, close to the banks, which moved him. On the polished surfaces of the boundless waves his thoughts slid easily and he never wearied of the sad sweetness of the setting. Then there were the deserted canals where the *stali* of gondoliers awoke echoes of yesteryear from the far, empty houses. And on beautiful summer evenings, reclining on black leather cushions, he often glided between the silent palaces, momentarily and splendidly renovated by the light of the moon. He felt with certainty that the city's soul and his own were merged, that it was not a coincidence that had led him to live there but the precise will of his Venetian ancestors, the Moro. For all well-born Romanians pretend to find in their family an aristocratic origin abroad, and etymology proved that the Moreano were descended from those Moro who gave a doge to Venice.

He had puerile distractions, such as dropping *lire* wrapped in paper near soldiers whose soft appearances tempted him. If they picked them up and kept them, he felt a great satisfaction, for he had a good heart. The pigeons of Saint Mark's Square interested him. With a distinguished gesture he distributed taming food to them, and rejoiced when their flapping wings surrounded his person. But a crowd usually gathered for this show, and Prince Mitrophane was unhappy at not being the sole audience for the pigeons.

Moreover, the oddity of his costumes (which he had harmonized with the polychrome marbles) brought attention and he appeared outside so infrequently that he was classified among the curiosities of Venice. He wore colored velvets and silks, his Byzantine face enhanced a painted, eternal smile under a thin and smooth moustache, his feet were clad in pointy boots, high heels clacking gracefully and anachronistically on the pavement as his lace-fringed, jewel-bedecked hands waved gently before him as if to ward off intruders. With his large, fixed eyes under his somewhat fugitive forehead, capped—according to the season—with a heavily-wrapped fur or straw hat, he trailed complicated perfumes when moving past. The gondoliers, accustomed to seeing him sitting apart on the steps, as near as possible to the water, gave him some consideration, for he spoke to them with a soft voice, and paid them nobly.

The futility of his existence was based around notable despair.

Despite the care he showed himself, the work of destructive aging continued in him with rapidity and no matter how skillfully he restored himself, he could not conceal its progress. A poignant sadness awaited him, often and from year to year more frequently, on returning from his sentimental or frivolous walks to the rooms where he loved only himself.

His reflection, the shadow of which he had been, awaited and addressed him with insidious speeches. "Look at you," he advised himself, "the miracle has come true. Your present form has been substituted, through force of will, with your past form. Look at yourself, and admire!"

He evoked, in the magnifying purple of the sunsets or in the flickering light of stellar candles, the elusive specter of his vanished youth, his forehead resting on the mirror's cold metal where the tin plating, like bitter flowers, defined the vain depths of that universe. And sometimes, during the soothing twilight of winter, he scrutinized the desolation of his bleached face, rendered more gloomy by the pallor of snow-covered rooftops. When the moon bathed the immobile objects in his chambers with unusual light, he anxiously interrogated the erased contours of the reflection, which he knew to be his own, where the traces of age were blurred. Alas, the memories of his younger years did not reappear as beautifully.

One night Orion, reflected in the narrow length of the canal, inclined his empty cross to the edge of the sky, his pale sword of stars obliquely fixed as if to the flank of some future messiah, and the prince thought that he himself might be the crucified man. The one who ironic Nature tortures in the flesh that it gave him and that he loved. Matter, for its children, is even more pitiless than the Spirit-God had been to his only Son.

At the reminder of intense and ephemeral joys, when formerly the singular seduction of his juvenile being would manifest itself to him, now only tears obscured his sight, and he sobbed.

"I who have loved only myself, and revealed to myself only my outer form, now find that the deforming finger of age has come to touch me, and I can not love myself anymore!"

He passionately hugged the inert frame and shouted:

"Come back, come back, O my youth, come back, my beauty. May my own fiery red mouth yet again rest upon my mouth, and may my soul, glimpsed in the terrible splendor of my dilated pupils, ascend from your magical abyss, O mirror, and once again swoon at itself!"

But from the murky water of his eyes the soul of love and grace no longer rose. It was agonized with his vanished youth, far, far away in the mists of the past, it agonized with the fleeting spring, with the dreams hatched around innocent cradles, with the flowers that adorn the virginity of the next wives.

And as he clasped his hands to his head and lamented, the image in front of him lamented as well, hideously tragic.

And it happened that, exhausted, he fell asleep on his knees, with his forehead touching the glass and his arms encircling the frame.

Then, from the marvelous mirror that sleep stretches towards us in a tired motion, arose the young man he had been, in apotheosis and shining with the tears he had shed, and he was so dazzled that he prostrated himself before the exhilarating vision of his ideal being.

Awakenings were atrocious. After the intoxicating enchantment of sumptuous dreams, the reality of his decay was so suddenly shown to him that, seized with terror, he slowly recoiled from the mirror and lurked in the darkest corner of the room, his eyes fixed on the dim form. And fixed so, before his tired retina, benevolent nuances of his distressing reflection started to move as his eyes remained locked, without seeing, without thinking, and he remained motionless.

Outside, disturbed by a passing boat, the water lapped gently.

VI

HALLUCINATIONS, borne from his dreams and restrained by the fantasies of kief, opium and later, cocaine, plagued him.

One hallucination, that became singular and domineering, was remarkable.

While ritual incense burned in precious censors under his mirrors, he walked slowly through the perfumed silence of his apartment while feeling he was journeying inside his own infinitely enlarged skull.

He dreamed his brain was divided into chapels, which he visited with pleasure. Here, the various faces of his being had their altars and before these hieratic effigies he prostrated himself devoutly.

After a time, though, the chapels fused and his mind widened into a vast and unique nave. He, alone in the evoked cathedral, continued his wanderings and was suffused with respect for the sanctity of the place.

After a long detour he stopped in the choir, which was lit up with long candles.

There, by means of a rich and subtle art, in vivid colors that leapt at him from a background of gold, was an image of the Trinity of the Virgin, the Prostitute and Love.

He was amazed at the triple figure which symbolized him, and he meditated aloud on the enigma he embodied.

"I am who is, who was, and who will be," he intoned.

And the specter of the Rosicrucian appeared at his side, clothed in a sacerdotal stole, and confirmed the statement with his own words, drawing the prince into an embrace with a dazzling silver and gold gesture.

"I am Death, I am Life, I am Love," the prince continued.

Voices—perhaps the monotonous cry of the gondoliers on the canal—floated down from the transept at his words.

"I am the one who is not.

"I am the one who would like to be.

"I am everybody and nobody."

He performed some genuflections. The Rosicrucian withdrew imperiously, as if to prepare some difficult mystery.

In a strident intonation, he resumed:

"I am Life and I die in all who call me.

"I am Death, and I am reborn in the unfulfilled desires of all who could not hold me back.

"I am Love, because all want me, all embrace me, all tear me apart. And I want all, I embrace all, I tear apart all.

"From Death to Life, from Life to Death, I am the tireless Ferryman."

The invisible voices resumed:

"You are Death, you are Life, you are the Virgin, the Prostitute."

"From one to the other, I am the Ferryman!"

"You are the Ferryman, you are Love!"

"I am Love!"

Then, before him, rose the indispensable and nefarious Rosicrucian who pointed with an imperious gesture to the arch of the choir where the fascinating Trinity appeared, encircled between the glow of long stained-glass windows.

He proclaimed: "In the untouchable, in the incorruptible, in the lone and immemorial mirror where the forces of the Past are reflected, consolidated and diversified, where the Present disintegrates, where the Future takes shape . . .

"Recognize yourself, son of the Past!

"Recognize yourself, harvest of Death, brother of the Present!

"From the Past to the Future, recognize yourself, determined Intermediate! Recognize yourself, Love!"

A murmur of desolate voices answered. And an immense mirror was suddenly substituted for the concave opacity of the wall. The glorious Trinity retreated into inaccessible spaces, becoming unrecognizable.

The Rosicrucian smirked: "Pursue yourself, reprove yourself, recognize yourself!"

And with great, but tiring and vain efforts, the unhappy man groaned:

"I am—I am Love. Oh, to look upon me again! I am the Virgin. Oh, take myself back, to kiss myself! . . . I am . . . Mitrophane, the poor, the dear Mitrophane."

He stammered, cried out . . .

VII

BY a curious anomaly, he had never consented to his portrait being painted. As a child he had opposed it energetically, with tears and lively agitation. Later his repugnance at a "capturing" of his features only increased, as he felt the physical sensation of a robbery when confronted with a sketching pencil or photographic camera. A fear haunted him that something of his countenance would disperse into the universe.

With time, as his face worsened, this fear clarified into a feeling which was at first ridiculous, but he did not try to defend himself from it. He became convinced that all his lost grace and beauty were really stolen from him and could be found elsewhere, so he did not hesitate to acquire any canvas or drawing in which he believed he recognized himself. He saw it as a returning of his property, and thought that perhaps this grouping of figurative totems around himself might eventually allow a recovery of his primal favors. Like so many magic pentacles, these representations were collected from everywhere with the hope that perhaps in them was concentrated the *idea* of his various external merits. The subtle Rosicrucian might not have disavowed such an interpretation of these questionable works of art, but the results did not answer the hopes of the unfortunate Prince Mitrophane. What had been stolen from him by some magical brush stroke he was unable to take back. He could not restore it and, what was worse, the pentacles were powerless to ward off new thefts that multiplied.

The evidence disillusioned him of the miraculous virtues of his little museum, but he did not doubt that he was the victim of very special depredations, which his knowledge allowed him to put under the term "spell."

He then turned his attention from images to authentic living examples. Meeting a passer-by who pleased him, his brain perverted the incident and he found himself irritated that the malicious stranger had appropriated some of his personal charm, and had the insolence to display it in front of him!

Having grown pusillanimous, and perhaps still aware of the peculiarity of such actions, he dared not accost the alleged thief. Instead he followed the stranger for a long time, with a gaze whose ardor might have been mistaken by an observer. When he finally returned home, he suffered fits of rage and pain during which he would have taken pleasure in killing.

It was especially after he had seen his youthful Trinity in that cathedral choir, and watched it recede and disappear into a mirror as if drawn away by an occult force, that he was seized with anguish. Convinced of the reality of his vision, he undertook to search within himself.

He haunted abandoned places, the spirit of solitude that still dwelt within him waiting to see the being (in whom he would find himself) emerge from the empty darkness. While the gondola slowly slid across the narrow, empty docks of the dead canals, his drowsy gaze of unspeakable despair scrutinized the darkness of the cellars through half-open doors. Sometimes, with a lazy shifting of his long, fringed eyelids, he glanced at those mysterious higher floors, where louvre windows were eternally closed, or peered at oblique boats in the lagoon whose colorful sails spread above foreigners. To hear from the populous quarters, not far away, the noisy song of life made him shudder. Perhaps, in that crowd whose sterile agitations disgusted him, there moved the one who he *must* join? He shook his head, reasoning, according to a wisdom that was peculiar to him, that every crowd was an assemblage of mediocrities. Elect Beings make a void around themselves, and they are discovered where others are not.

On clear, moonlit nights passers-by projected recognizable silhouettes onto his shimmering, liquid pathway.

At odd hours he ventured to the main piazza, or he would sit near the Bridge of Sighs on the flat steps, almost flush with the waves. His glowing, jewel-encrusted hands supported his motionless head and, bent in two but not without elegance in his dark velvet costume, he waited with a heavy heartbeat for *the unknown one* to arrive. The sound of lingering footsteps made him tremble and the shadows that brushed against him warned of the uselessness of his emotion.

Moved by the vanity of his pursuits, a sob quietly grew in his throat while the voices of the hours descended to the sea's surface from the slender bell-towers. With a rather lamentable smile he pointed an imploring and scintillating little finger towards the stars. High in the sky, they smiled on the cupolas and palaces of dreams, and were not in sympathy with his grief at all.

VIII

ON a certain day his hands involuntarily twitched, a small cry rose from his throat, and he turned extremely pale. The obliging gondolier, believing the prince was fainting, stopped rowing, but Mitrophane signaled him to land.

They were at the opening of the Lido Pass, and the eddy of the flow rocked them. The sky, where the sun was setting, was a diaphanous cloth of incarnadine silk and straw, thin clouds tracing a network of gold. Behind them, in the pale green water streaked by purple and orange stripes, the city sprouted the pink petals of its palaces, between which stood the long white pistils of spires, topped with golden points.

Jaded by the magnificence of the spectacle, Prince Mitrophane did not linger in sterile contemplation. Sobered, he quickly moved to a rather shabby looking shack, where fishermen were drinking thick red wine from coarse glasses. As he sat down they made a place for him and, in the sweet Venetian dialect, started a conversation with this stranger, whose clothing and manner seemed of English origin.

Contrary to what one might think, he responded rather easily to their advances as the society of working people did not displease him. He enjoyed viewing their sturdiness and, like all who are weak, he felt he could draw strength from their virile company. Moreover, the simplicity of their souls contrasted with the complication of his own, and in the midst of them he took some pride in who he was.

At their questioning, he condescended in his lisping voice to instruct them of his nationality. But his explanations, a little prolix and not devoid of boastfulness, went over their heads and they decided that he must be the son of the Queen of Turkey.

After a few minutes, as he was growing restless, he finally inquired about a young sailor he had spied just before disembarking. At the moment when the gondola was lining up against the boom, the young man had disappeared. Was he not part of their company?

Deliberately composing a face of indifference, he waited for their answer, gripped with a fear that he may have been hallucinating. But at his description of the sailor they interrupted him, laughing and smiling:

"You will see him, lord, you will see him!" they exclaimed, gay from his generous gift of wine. And they called, "Nesta! Nesta!"

Since the sailor seemed in no hurry to show up a man went to fetch him and, after some conversation enlivened with the sounds of kisses, the messenger reappeared, holding a young lady by the hand.

"Here is the sailor!" the man said cheerfully as he presented her.

The swarthy faces were delighted with the stupefaction of the noble, foreign lord. Nesta, animated by their cheerfulness, gracefully came over to Mitrophane and asked whether he was disappointed.

The prince, his head lowered a little, rolled from under his half-closed eyelids a sly and singularly attentive look towards the young lady. Despite the fresh breeze from the open sea, drops of sweat beaded on his forehead. Having taken from his pocket an overly-perfumed silk handkerchief, he wiped his head carefully, so as not to disturb the established order of his rarefied hairstyle. Nesta noticed the lace on his wrists and the jewels on his fingers, and praised them.

He smirked and nodded in agreement.

Nevertheless, his voluble neighbors narrated to him why the *ragazzo* of a moment ago had changed into a *ragazza*. Nesta served as cabin apprentice for her father, a fisherman like the others, and it was more convenient when at sea for her to put on male clothes. Moreover, she loved wearing them, "is that not so, Nesta?"

She agreed convincingly and declared, nonetheless, that it was more suitable that she serve in woman's dress when at the *trattoria*.

So saying, she stood before Prince Mitrophane with a rather haughty air, her little brown fist on her hip, her intrepid head thrown to one side. And he said to her:

"You look like a disguised teenage boy."

Then, while the satisfied fishermen exhaled vigorous puffs of the Virginia tobacco that the prince had distributed appreciably, he begged her in an altered voice to kindly do him the favor of donning the sailor's suit again.

"I like you so in it," he said.

She taunted him:

"And now, do you not like me anymore?"

He blushed, stammered:

"You cannot understand."

And as she hesitated, he persuaded her by promising a sufficient reward.

The evening scattered mauve light over the water and pale roses near the horizon, the clouds enclosing puddles of green sky. The nearby Adriatic whispered irregularly, and isolated songs hovered, like flights of sad birds, over the sands of the Lido. In the lagoon, the distant islands were falling asleep. The springtime atmosphere was both feverish and melancholy.

One after the other, the fishermen took leave of Prince Mitrophane, thanking him cordially.

While he waited, moved somewhat by the great shimmering spaces of the evening's sorrow, intoxicated by wine he was not accustomed to and distracting himself from excited passions, he complacently remembered an old police order concerning Venetian courtesans. The exact text of the regulation escaped him, but they were forbidden to wear men's clothing in malicious pursuit of attracting reprehensible debauchees. Evoked by this reminiscence, his bawdy former days unrolled before him in a spill of silks, velvet, jewels, music and perfumes, a learned procession of his vices and his deceptions. He moistened his lips, which ardor had dried, with wine brought to his mouth by his fevered hands.

As this heady and deliciously terrifying phantasmagoria of past voluptuousness paraded through his memory,

Nesta reappeared at the threshold of the shack, his hopeful figure of desired satisfaction. And suddenly, in her, he recognized himself.

No longer an uncertain, fleeting vision glimpsed while the gondola slid along the muddy shore, instead she was a firm, graspable reality.

This fair-skinned ephebe, with large blue eyes under bright eyebrows and a red beret proudly poised on rich brown curls, her set mouth a red and tasty summation, was him as he had once been. He scrutinized every detail of her face, and found in it an irreproachable reproduction of his youthful features. That young man's—or young girl's—pose, leaning slightly on the left hand so that the head bowed to the same side, while the right hip protruded, was his. She had the analogous disdainful lips, and her loins were girded with scarlet wool, which as a child he had desired but which had been refused him as vulgar.

He had to examine her at leisure. It was urgent that he should recover himself.

In an instant, mad desire rose in his eyes, a desire which she did could not mistake. Shuffling a little, she came to him uncertainly—a young boy or girl?—in her jacket and sailor's collar, opening on the tanned nakedness of an exquisite, sexless breast.

Her trousers of thick blue cloth were rolled up to the knees. Thus her calves, which were tanned and muscular, remained as bare as her feet were. These appeared well arched, with neat toes. Her thin hands emerged from thinner sleeves, the arms satisfyingly muscled under the wool.

No doubt, Nesta had endured the imposition of many fantasies akin to Prince Mitrophane's, and he had decided to pay extra, in anticipation of future events, because she was pleasingly scented and her clothes did not smell of the fishing boat's hold.

But at his brief word she gave a little shudder of fear and suddenly backed away from him, for the hand he had laid on her shoulder was that of a master.

She looked at him askance. In the twilight, his sharp, hard profile was unusual and disturbing, with its makeup and tints no longer illuminated by daylight.

He understood, and made himself meek and tractable.

"Come with me!" he implored.

"Where do you live?"

He named the canal to her, pointing to the house.

She shrugged, looking around with indifference.

"I do not have time," she said, "and it will rain soon."

She said this as if it was a comment on good weather to come.

He pulled a ruby from his ring finger and slipped it into her hand.

"I have others," he insinuated.

The jewel seduced her. With audacity, she interrogated him:

"You will give me gold?"

"Certainly!"

"Right now?"

He fumbled in his wallet.

"Here!"

"Wait for me!"

She returned to the interior of the hut, where the volunteer gondoliers had retreated. No doubt the discussion was reassuring, since she soon reappeared.

"Do you like me?" she asked and whispered special words in his ears while embracing him.

He dismissed this:

"Come. Follow me."

As they departed, shadows appeared at the windows of the twilit houses and calling voices followed their gondola.

They slipped through the funerary black water, between the drowned heads of pilings. They moved away from that joyous space where flared the wide curve of reflected light from the Giudecca between the confused masses of buildings and entered the sinister side of Murano, facing the Isle of Tombs, a maze of mostly abandoned canals. As her companion did not speak or move, but only gazed at her with strangely fixed eyes, Nesta felt fear.

IX

BUT when she entered the apartment, her fear turned into respect. The permanent scent of incense, and some other subtle perfume she did not know, moved her religiously. The heavy hangings and thick carpets, which smothered the sound of footsteps, made her speak as softly as if she were in a sacred place. In the room at the end of the alcove, above the wide divan where rose the mirror of mystery, she was even tempted to kneel and she made the sign of the cross.

He watched her and perceived each of her feelings, as if he dwelt inside her head. Under an attentive but reserved exterior he concealed his extravagant joy at having so near, in his home and at his disposal, his own stolen youth. He laughed inside to see himself now a woman and, despite the inverted gender, dressed in the attractive masquerade of a sailor suit quite similar to one he had once worn, and so even more desirable. Ha! He was going to seize his property, dizzyingly possess it and fall into red abysses of pleasure! . . . He would have his revenge for such long waits and great despairs . . . He would knead flesh, restore himself to life, and—Gods!—reflect in such prodigious human mirrors! . . . But, hush . . . it was not necessary to frighten the child with sudden manifestations when he had previously been so gloomy, even as those presences rejoiced in the high glass.

And with feline precaution he approached Nesta, fingertips daring to knead the skin of her neck, passing his hand so lightly that it barely grazed her hair. Quivering, he moved away and then returned, cajoling. He, the previously silent man, condescended to gallant speeches.

However, she was acclimating to this awesome luxury. The candles, hung high in the massive bronze candelabra, ceased to evoke in her simple imagination the splendors of tabernacles. The wool of the carpets tickled her bare feet and she was emboldened into small bursts of laughter. Her natural childishness, enhanced by some depravity, gained the upper hand. She annoyed her strange lover by expressing pleasantly lascivious attitudes. While in the bathroom, having discovered the powder and blush boxes, she desired to make up and primp like him, but she aborted this attempt. Rather, she instinctually grasped that what suited her host were her own crude charms, her bachelor-like looks. This adventure, which she had dared many times with others no less extravagant in the poor rooms at the Lido or in a propitiously rocking gondola, amused her now, in this refined decor of carpets, mirrors, and lights. And this polite, if certainly not beautiful, gentleman knew how to be lovable and his fingers sparkled with tempting rings.

At the supper table, she was quite at ease. Despite his precious sorrows, Prince Mitrophane was a gourmand who took great care with his buffet, and his wines were of unquestionable merit.

Nesta had an appetite, and drank wine with the awkward grace of an ephebe curious about worldly usage. He, his eyes glowing, looked upon his tasty morsel with satisfaction, but he restrained himself from touching.

When she saw the *mousse d'un moscato d'Asti*, she brightened and was bold enough to give little pats to the enamel of his princely cheek, asking if she frightened him as he had not favored her with even the least kiss. In a supreme passion of joy and fury, he was on the point of taking her head, which was his, in his two hands and crushing it . . . she only perceived the tawny glow of his eyes, and rejoiced at feeling desired.

And, after having their coffee in small silver cups, they sampled liqueurs. Nesta also wished to smoke an elegant pipe of tobacco and mix in a little *kief*, which her aristocratic and scented friend smoked in slow puffs.

Mitrophane encouraged her. The experiment succeeded and, delighted by the new perfume, she smoked immoderately.

Dazed, she rose from the seat where she had flung herself with her arms behind her head, and zigzagged through the rooms, just like a young, slightly drunk, sailor.

Here his lust, cleverly tamed thus far, rose powerfully and he followed closely on her heels. They were in the alcove now, and he threw her on the divan.

Mechanically, she began undressing, but he stopped her.

"Not yet!" he ordered.

Strangely mastering himself, he brought into the little room all the candelabras, all of the lamps he possessed. Their flames displayed dazzling and disparate light. Under the multiple rays, objects became animated with an unusual life.

He carefully locked the door. On small censors lit in front of the various mirrors he burned incense, and soon the brightness of the lights dimmed in the mystical smoke.

She was a little surprised, but vaguely charmed by this staging. In truth, she did not know exactly where she was. The initial impression of a chapel again came to her, and she stammered words of prayer. And as her dazzled eyes grew tired, she closed them. Immediately, she was asleep . . .

A sharp pain woke her.

She screamed. Leaning over her, she caught a glimpse of a sneering mask:

"It's nothing at all. *My* lips, I just wanted *my* lips."

Furious at the unexpected attack, her mouth bleeding from a bite, she struggled with all her strength and pushed him away. But singularly strong, he grabbed her and eagerly sucked the flowing blood.

And with a rapid movement of his hands, he tore her collar, stripped her of her tunic and her *tricot*.

Dazed, she let herself be handled roughly as this.

Her young and firm nakedness suddenly revealed, he cried in a clamor of triumph:

"All mine, all for me!"

His embrace was cruel, and she groaned in pain.

In a moment of relaxation, she escaped his abuse, insulting him. But he picked her up, gripped steel fingers around her neck and shouted:

"Your voice, yes, I need *my* voice! Cry for me, moan for me, sing for *me*!

"My teeth! I want my teeth, bite me with *my* teeth!

"My hair! I demand the rejuvenated wonder of *my* hair!

"And *my* blood! And *my* skin! And *my* flesh, and *all* that you took from *me*!"

He shook her furiously, and she struggled in vain against the embrace of those little hands that had become so formidable. She dragged him to the door, attempting to flee in mortal terror. Candelabras were upset, they flickered, fell, and one of them struck a mirror, scattering shards of glass over them. She realized then that her life was over.

His fingers squeezed harder. She convulsed and a cry of horror froze in her wide open mouth. Then there was a crack, and her limbs relaxed suddenly, her hands opened, loose, and her head hung down on her chest.

He exulted and, stumbling through the disorder of broken objects, he carried the limp body to the divan and rolled with it onto the cushions, proclaiming:

"I am no longer the Virgin, I am no longer the Prostitute. I have regained Love, I am only Love, the Absolute, the omnipotent Love, as in my person two sexes are mingled!"

A spasm of frightful laughter clenched his teeth, and he frantically kissed her warm, helpless flesh.

Then suddenly, as he brought his head nearer to her own, drawing his own eyes to her dead gaze, he gave a cry of distress:

"The mirrors are broken! *My* eyes, *my* mirrors! What have I done to you! I do not see myself anymore in you! *My* eyes, O *my* beautiful mirrors. O me, dear me, all of me! Poor Mitrophane! My eyes, my sweet mirrors!"

He cried abundantly, tears ruining his makeup, and in a desolate gesture he scratched his face with his jeweled fingers.

Naked and bent over the edge of the couch, lay Nesta, her head thrown back, her dilated pupils absent of any gaze.

One by one the candles and lamps went out. The darkness grew. And then Mitrophane fell asleep, continuing to sob, like a sorrowful child . . .

ANNTJÖ-MÖ

ON the whole Frisian island of Juist there was no older old woman than Mother Anne, Anntjö-mö, as she was called in their language. Stunted, folding her body if she walked into a gust of wind, her creased and ruddy face buried in a tall, clean, white cap, she was seen in the morning going for provisions. Clad in a very old brown dress with white flowers, her big bag on her arm, she trundled along the brick streets of the village, through which an incessant wind carries the fine sand of the dunes. Striking her cane on the threshold of low fishermen's houses to announce herself, she chatted abundantly, inquiring after the boy who had just entered the navy, an eldest daughter in service to wealthy people on the continent, a grandfather and his rheumatism; and she gave advice with the cunning and mischievous looks of an old scoundrel, as she shook her head. She was welcomed everywhere for, as an octogenarian midwife, she was much like a mother to them all, young or old. The islanders, too, being very cautious by nature, thought she might be a little like a witch, and wanted to avoid attracting evil spells on themselves by ill-will.

The round of the households finished, Anntjö-mö turned her head aside as she passed the church, because like all the coastal population she despised the temple and abhorred the pastor, remaining pagan at her roots. She crossed the large deserted place where rough turf grows in little tufts, and in spite of the wind that raged there and set her *cornette* all crooked, reached the isolated stall that leant against a row of dunes, where a grocer has been established to sell goods. She would buy a honey pie, a slice of sausage, or a quarter of a liter of brandy. Then, having placed on the counter (not without sighing) her nickel coins, she returned home, her head wobbling and eyes flashing, mumbling incomprehensible words, and greeted fearfully along her way by the children with wheat-blond hair and porcelain eyes, lewd and shy in their movements, who played silently in arid gardens or on the muddy beach.

If the weather was fine, at low tide she took the long way home, skirting the village by the coast, sinking to her ankles in the black mud revealed by the ebb of the waters of the "Watt", the wide channel of the Wadden Sea which separates the island from the mainland. There she picked up mussels and crabs which she carefully put in a wicker basket and then sold to the innkeeper near her house. Raising her skirt very high, she waddled slowly and cautiously in the slimy mud, moving past the tipped schooners, her old, slender figure outlined in a black silhouette on the sparkling dunes, like some wreck that had suddenly come alive . . .

Having finished her harvest, she easily, despite her load, climbed the embankment which, in the summer, was carpeted with a multitude of small, delicate yellow flowers, and returned to her house, not venturing out any more that day . . .

Her house was an isolated cottage, located at the end of the village. A tiny garden, enclosed by a dwarf hedge, separated her from the high road. The garden was brick-lined, planted spottily with squares of marigolds and carnations. And it was one of Anntjö-mö's constant pre-occupations to drive out the chickens and replace the red bricks which, simply resting on the shifting sand, constantly moved from the alignment imposed on them.

The entrance doorway was so low that Antjö-mö filled it entirely with her form. The four rooms of the little house were very small, pierced with tiny windows at knee height, and the ceiling crossed with joists which were easily touched by hand. These rooms were scrupulously clean and crowded with curious furniture, almost fantastic in the diffused light that the narrow windows allowed to filter in: old, massive, oddly turned tables and stiff, heavy armchairs in carved wood, too tall for the little space and contrasting with the straw chairs and a couch made from branches. On the walls were exotic shelves with large pink Indian shells. On an antique sideboard, throwing an unexpectedly cheerful note, were cups of red or green porcelain, saucers, ordinary vases and some mismatched Dutch Delftware from a ship once wrecked on the large, inhospitable beach whose roaring enveloped the house in a monotonous and continuous complaint. In a kind of alcove, behind Indian curtains with brown arabesques, lay an immense bed of dried kelp, covered with coarse cloth and with three or four cushions piled up. In all the time that Antjö-mö had slept there, her light body had molded it in the middle, like a groove in a mattress.

But during the day, and only in the winter, Anntjö-mö lived in her rooms and slept during the night for the least possible time, because she was afraid of sleep, afraid of falling asleep so deeply that she would not wake up anymore . . .

She spent her day watering her barnyard, weeding her meager beds and conversing with the big black rooster who sang on her window at dawn. In the afternoon, having emptied her small carafe of brandy, most often she sat under the awning with her grandson, Claas the idiot, and vaguely looked at the horizon for whole hours, her lips moving as if she told were telling herself endless stories of the past . . .

She did not see the flat line of the continent opposite, low under the gray sky, nor the yellow water whipped with white foam which slowly ascended into the Watt, nor the soft curvature of the grassy shore. She did not smell the honey of the little flowers scattered profusely in this corner of the island . . . but she shuddered with pleasure when the dry, salty wind drove the sand of the great dunes over her. A tawny glow lit up her eyes when it was blowing up a storm and the waves, breaking on the other side of the island, could be heard like deafening detonations.

A long time ago, in the evenings when the North Sea rose angrily and leaped as if to bury the narrow island under its mighty mass, great fires were lit on the coast, treacherous fires which attracted ships in distress . . . And when they were stranded on the sandbanks the shipwrecked ones were pushed mercilessly back into the long, curved waves, with the help of long, fanged poles . . . The treasures brought by the ocean were shared fraternally between islanders, debris of all kinds rattling among the corpses. Sometimes gold, beautiful and striking pieces of gold stamped with old effigies which she still kept in a secret drawer . . . Back then there was plenty, the legitimate stripping of a stranger who is always an enemy, the cowardly freedom . . .

She sneered, thinking of those remote times that the imbibed alcohol revived sharply and more temptingly in her memory . . .

And then suddenly she became tender, because in the cemetery of those years she would meet again with her husband, and her sons, and her daughters, and her grandchildren; all dead, all disappeared, either in the Ocean that she hated, or as a result of slow and mysterious illness, as if a curse weighed on her family . . . And this old woman with the sneaky eye and fleeting gait, was taken sometimes by a tumultuous love for those who had belonged to her and who were no longer and, hidden from all, a gasp of pain like a sob rose to her throat and shook the flabby skin of her neck . . .

Of all her numerous offspring, only one remained, and he was stupid.

She did not fail to love her Claas, that tall boy of twenty, son of her youngest daughter, since he had the robust neck and muscular limbs of his grandfather, but also mostly because he was the last, the only one left. But his stupid laugh, his inertia, his raw animal appetite revolted her anyway, and she often beat him like a wicked animal.

Then he took refuge in some dark corner, growling, and threw looks at his grandmother full of vague threats. Most of the time, however, during the day he would stand near her, for solitude made him anxious and, like a dog, he humbly stretched out at her feet at sunset, his big clumsy hands playing in the sand, or painstakingly moving the small single bricks back into their straight line. He terrified the chickens with horrifying cries, throwing himself into their enclosure and sometimes, in a fit of ferocity, seizing one of them, slaughtering it, and laughing at seeing the blood drain away . . .

Wasn't he dead too, after all, when he came into the world? It would have been better to be alone, all alone, than to have to feed that useless mouth, to see that silly smile, a perpetual caricature of his grandfather's wide laugh . . . With impatience she rose to her feet, moving to and fro with her quick, dry footsteps, looking in the rooms through the windows, roaming the henhouse, trying to hinder some traveler on the road with talk; then, tired, returning to sit in her usual place, soon joined by her grandson . . .

Oh, those long summer evenings when the sun, setting late in a haze of blood, prolonged to infinity the gloomy dreams of the past! And those long winter nights when dawn did not come, when the wind and rain mixed with snow whipped the cottage, as the frightened idiot crept near her, she who was no longer sleeping but dared not to get up yet, because outside it was dark and cold.

And that joy, always felt at daybreak when the air is barely transparent, to cross the threshold of the door and to mumble words, as in an incantation, which attracted the confident animals, which made them hurry around you to have their food and be caressed . . . But Claas stealthily followed his grandmother, and his sluggish look that she felt fixed on herself embarrassed her, exasperated her . . .

✳

Now that morning, the summer sun rose with an unusual splendor for these sad places. Its golden disk slowly rose above the desolate shore of the continent, and sheaves of light vaulted the pure sky, slid on the shimmering surface of the sea, and shone silver on the dunes. The red roofs of the village gleamed and the lost hovel of Anntjö-mö, in these glorious beams, seemed a very old thing, ashamed to be dark and decrepit in the eternal rejuvenation of nature . . .

That morning, at an hour when it usually showed some life, the house of Anntjö-mö had an unusual air of abandonment. The old woman had not shown herself yet, the little door had not grated familiarly as a signal of deliverance for the barnyard, prelude of a great agitation, and marigolds and carnations hung their heads sadly, waiting in vain for the morning watering.

As the sun continued to rise, thin, white clouds flew across the sky, a faint mist spread like a muslin cloth on the Watt, and the yellow line of the continent disappeared. The sun became pale again, as on previous days, and while the village returned to life in an atmosphere suffused with sadness, and the dunes were losing their luster and dull profile, it drew a sinuous line on the horizon with an air of boredom.

The house of Anntjö-mö seemed as if it would remain closed forever when finally, at about seven o'clock, the door opened and Claas appeared. The brilliant day seemed to dazzle him, for he was rubbing his eyes with a gloomy air, and his long sleep had weighed down his legs. Having remained some time unresolved on the threshold, he decided to go forward and left the garden. Shading his eyes with both hands, he looked around him. No one was on the high road at that hour—when passers-by are scarce—and there was no one on the beach. He made an angry gesture. No doubt his grandmother had gone out at dawn and had gone far away, as she sometimes did, to the farm at the very end of the island, forgetting to wake him up and prepare food. Without thinking of going to the old woman's room, since she was never there at that hour, he re-entered the house and went to the cupboard that held provisions. He shook it violently, as he was very excited, and broke the rusty, weak lock. He found some crusts of bread, a piece of cake, and rations of meat, which he eagerly devoured and, having discovered a half-liter of brandy, he hastily drank it with delight, as an exquisite and forbidden thing . . . Then, aimlessly and already a little drunk, he went to the henhouse, drove out all its inhabitants and laughed a lot at seeing the chickens fluttering and bristling their feathers, while the rooster pecked and pinched the legs of the stragglers. Tired of throwing stones at them, and having run out of breath, he found it amusing to trample the flowerbeds and dislocate the assembly of bricks. Tired, he sat on the bench beneath his grandmother's windows, his legs heavy, his arms dangling, his naked chest and neck pleasantly tickled by the rays of the sun. The chickens, with a busy air, came to peck at the ground beneath his feet, and he let them go, smiling smugly at them. The ground seemed like it rolled gently, the surrounding objects wobbled strangely, and he was about to fall asleep . . .

A loud moan, an indistinct call, pulled him from his torpor. He turned around limply. The complaint was renewed, more strongly, coming from the old woman's room. His grandmother was not out? Very intrigued by this, he pushed at the unclosed windows and looked, but his eyes were dazzled by the external light, and floating gleams prevented him from distinguishing anything. Awkwardly, then, he stepped over the window ledge, risking the chance of pulling the frame out with his shoulders, and then, very astonished, found himself in the room. A little frightened, he stopped, briefly worried that he had done something wrong, and crouched in the corner like a dog who fears blows. But when the old woman began to whine again, he straightened up with sudden resolve and, knocking over one of the great armchairs, went to the alcove, from which he drew aside the curtains.

A wide beam of light fell obliquely on Anntjö-mö's convulsed face. Her white hair, in stiff locks, spread from behind her neck, whiter than the cushions, making the skin of the old woman appear more shriveled and tanned than ever, in contrast. A little scum had settled on the corners of her mouth, horribly deformed and stammering brief syllables, while her eyes remained very alive, moving quickly in their orbits. The sheets fell into rigid folds on the motionless body and her withered, mummy-like hand, with long nails of dubious color, squeezed the wooden slats of the bed. Anntjö-mö, struck in the night by an attack of apoplexy, was dying.

Claas looked at her with interest and curiosity. He could not understand why his grandmother was still in bed, and her hoarse wailing worried him. He paced to and fro by the bedside, shaking her as if to urge her to get up, bending over her, approaching her contracted mouth with his big, clownish head to understand what she wanted. And he only grasped these words: "Head, head hurts." She wanted to speak, but she had lost the memory of words and found only these. At last he thought he had discovered something to relieve her, and staggered out of the room.

A few moments later he reappeared, holding in his hand a bowl which contained barley soup. As his idiot brain was tortured only by the desire to eat, a reflection had emerged: if his grandmother was suffering, it was because she was hungry . . . and he attempted to satisfy her. Soaking a piece of bread in the soup, he introduced it, as he had done with geese, into the throat of the old woman, who grumbled and rolled terrible eyes. With a snap, Anntjö-mö's jaws closed on Claas's index finger, cutting deeply. The latter hastily withdrew his bloody hand, uttering a cry of pain, and looked with hatred at his grandmother, who had begun to stammer: "Head, head hurts."

What diabolical idea of vengeance emerged from the tortuous brain of Claas? In what obscure folds of his being had his past grudges hidden, terrible in their sudden blossoming? Did he understand, under the exciting effect of the alcohol, that the old woman was in his power, and that the moment for action had come? His eyebrows were frowning, and an evil smile pinched his lips.

"In the head," he murmured, "in the head;—come, I know how to fix your head . . ." And he ran out, laughing loudly and stridently.

He returned as quickly as he had left, holding a heavy object in his hands. The door having remained open behind him, a great clarity filled the room, and on the white background of the wall, the dying woman projected a shadow of frightening sharpness. Perched on the narrow window, the familiar rooster stood in a fighting attitude, waving its red comb and standing on its spurs.

Claas stood in front of Anntjö-mö, whose fright magnified her eyes immeasurably, brandishing with both hands a huge hammer: "For the head!" he said.

A beam of light—a sound like crackling dry wood—a deep moan and a convulsive movement under the sheets, that was all: Anntjö-mö was gone. On her forehead, between her two eyes, a thin crack appeared with a few drops of blood, while the hammer rolled into the space beside the bed.

Exhausted by this effort, vanquished by drunkenness, Claas fell to the ground and soon fell deeply asleep. And while a livid pallor invaded the grandmother's face, whose widened eyes kept a sinister expression of terror, the grandson's face grew rosy, as in children whose sleep is calm and without dreams, and his fair hair was gilded by the midday sun . . . However, on the window, the black cock flapped its wings and sounded a triumphal fanfare.

THE OTHER

PERHAPS she was delirious, because in a monotonous but somehow very sweet voice she said:

"It is red, the flowing blood, hot and red—it is purple—and now it is black, the blood that flows, because the night is black, it is black and cold, because the night is cold, and the thick wool of the carpet has not been able to drink it all, for it has flowed abundantly, blood . . . blood . . ."

She was smiling, shaking her blonde curls lightly and looking at us without any fear or surprise. She half-raised herself from the bed and continued:

"It's not me—it's the *other* one who is the cause, you know, the *Other* whose blood has also flowed . . . the *Other*, do you remember? You do not remember, You do not want to believe me, and yet it's the truth!"

A little anxiety disturbed her pale and charming face, while her blue eyes went to the half-open shutters, grazed by the oblique rays of the declining sun.

"Listen," she said, "before the sun has set, for afterwards I *know* I will have to remain silent. I will tell you everything. You will see that it is the *Other*. Listen."

She had fallen back on her cushions, and with a cautious and persuasive inflection of voice she continued to speak. Had it not been for the strange expression in her gaze, worried by invisible objects she was discovering beyond the fog formed by the opaque walls and the heaviness of the curtains, she would have seemed lucid and tranquil, as in her stronger days of old.

"Before seeing *it*, I doubt I had a soul, for no definite memory has remained of my childhood. There was a something vaguely fearsome blocking my first youth and every time I looked at its mystery I felt the same anxiety that comes when plunging from a boat into the dark depths of the ocean at nightfall, searching for answers . . . From the day I met him, my life began. The pressure of his hand molded a heart for me, his words created a soul for me—yes, a soul, timid and confused at first but by degrees strengthened, which said to my heart that it beat for Emmanuel, and that Emmanuel was my predestined husband. At this idea I shuddered, and a violent and disturbing joy passed over my being like a hot summer breeze. And the mysterious future appeared to me like a great sunny plain, rising to magical horizons.

"Unknowingly yielding to my attractive desire, Emmanuel married me without loving me. Could he love me, since he always loved the *other*, Norah, his first wife, dead for years . . . ?

"Oh, how he had loved her! I saw her in his eyes, when he lay asleep and seductive. When he smiled, it was because the dead one had passed before him and recited bewitching words from afar, and as she vanished into the golden transparency of glorious morning, the reflections

86

on his face of the illusory happiness that had visited him weakened.

"In the evening, when great fires lit up the sky and empurpled the sea, especially in the evening she was with him, so closely it was as if she touched even me. And when the shadows fell, he seemed to suffer the prolonged charm of the failing light and the night invading the waters and the sky. Motionless on a divan, I heard him sigh because in the darkness he contemplated her more alive, but no less elusive . . .

"But I, who understood all that, was not jealous, not jealous at all because in becoming his wife I knew that the *other* would continue to embrace him. So often he had talked to me about her, and so passionately! I only wanted to live near him, to discreetly envelop him with tenderness, and with the smile of my presence to dissipate his somber moods.

"With a slight step I came to him when his vague glances lingered complacently on inaccessible infinities. Putting my hand on his icy forehead, he seemed to shake off a domineering dream and stared at me with delirious eyes from which disorder soon dissipated. Then a shade of pleasure pinked his cheeks and he passed his arm around my waist. Through the tall open windows I showed him the sparkling day, the triumphal blue of the sea, the curve of the red rocks and the lustrous and undulating vegetation that crowned them, the cork oaks and stone pines, the long cypresses and the mimosas, and closer, the camellias and rhododendrons, the baskets of roses . . . Exalting himself to the motionless and changing splendor of things, he completely forgot his preceding visionary drowsiness and became enchanted by the warmth of the air and the grace of nature. The flowers especially captivated him. He stroked them with the hands of a lover, examining the complex beauty, admiring the veins of the petals, the grace of the corolla, the coquetry of the stamens. He imagined them with countenances in which he discerned smiles, worries, tender languor, and even gloomy thoughts. He caressed them with his fingertips, saw them vibrating under his touch, leaned over their fragrant calyxes intoxicating himself with their aroma and, rising, kissed me as he would have kissed a trembling rose at the end of its stem . . . Dragging me further out on our walks, he sat between the myrtles, at the end of the rocks overhanging the singing water. Hot exhalations emanated from the sunlit earth and the promontories were veiled with a red hot haze. Under the cracked soil, insects whispered. He was silent. But, from the unconscious pressure of his hand, I guessed that his melancholy dream was very far away, and the ambient calm penetrated into him. He lost himself in the vastness of the marvelous horizons, by degrees he merged with the sky and the sea, cradling them in a sumptuous expanse, and so for hours a voluptuousness of oblivion and static life numbed him.

"At other times, when the rainy days blurred the surroundings and made the silent dwelling gray, that dear vision attached itself to him like clouds to the mountains and proved just as irremovable and saddening. Then, I went to sit at the piano in the next room. My hands glided over the keys and softly I played arpeggio chords as on a harp, strange and primitive melodies which seemed to float in from somewhere else and scatter in tears our most secret sorrows. And he cried. I did not see him, but I knew he was crying, because all his feelings had become mine, his sorrows were my sorrows, and in our sleep the same dreams visited us both . . . Kadi, the familiar cat, left his master and snuck into my room, jumping with a soft leap onto the instrument, wrapping her huge tail around her paws and considering me fixedly, as if demanding I not interrupt my playing. She laid in front of me quietly, imposing as an idol. Her oblong pupils narrowed more and her irises became ever greener, her stern look seeming to say, "He is suffering, and you can not help it." Then, upset by the constant melody, she suddenly jumped to the ground and ceaselessly mewed, as if regretting she had not brought her beloved master along. Under the disintegrating influence of these sounds, the haunting visions dissipated and as the cold shadows of the night grew longer, a little contentment penetrated our tired hearts in contrast . . .

"The days were similar and idle, filled with my love, filled with his memories, and the monotony of our existence was wearying neither for him nor for me. Moreover, I had developed a new feeling. Since I could not soften the incurable nostalgic love that Emmanuel was suffering from, I must share it. Since our engagement he had rarely spoken of Norah, so it was left to me to first pronounce her name. Didn't she approach me and, through calls which I distinctly perceived, incite me to evoke her person in our languid conversations? I obeyed the calls, and immediately Emmanuel's eyes shone brighter, the muscles of his face relaxed, and his gratitude for my tender interest in the dead vibrated in the sound of his voice.

"I frequently asked him about Norah, and the silent sadness which impregnated our dwelling dissipated. I learned *her* habits, *her* preferences, *her* particular thoughts. And with every detail that was revealed something answered faintly in me, a vague reminiscence or déjà-vu awakened in my being, and I understood more intimately what Emmanuel said to me than he himself thought he imparted. A strange sympathy, made of shared memories of who knows what, pulled me towards she who was no longer and who I knew so well, despite never having seen her at all. I preferred to spend time in the rooms she had loved, finding the refined and discreet luxury with which she had adorned them to my taste. The colors that were pleasant to her were also my favorite colors. Like her, I dressed in long robes of red velvet, whose proud trails unfolded like scarlet snakes on the Oriental carpets. I was about the same height as she was and shared her deportment and haughty manner, to the point that when I emerged from the depths of the vast apartments, Emmanuel thought that the very dead had arisen from the depths of the past, approaching him as impassively beautiful as before and just as dangerous, but younger . . . The dream of the previous years faded, making way for a new, tangible vision, but until I neared he eagerly contemplated me, saying: "Norah! Norah!", then smiled with pleasure and kissed my neck.

"We sat side by side, speaking phrases that must have come from *their* mouths years before. He rose, paced back and forth through the austere library, rolling fine blonde cigarettes between his fingers, blue smoke passing before my eyes in a fragrant fog. He even sketched plans for the future and feverishly developed them, as if a new need for activity had seized him. Then, suddenly, he would fall back into his habitual silence. I read the books *she* had read, or I worked on *her* unfinished embroidery of marvelous silks. And when once more the night advanced, the day withdrawing from the room like warmth leaving a corpse, whatever I held in my hand, book or embroidery, dropped away and I knew not what distress squeezed my throat, what unfulfilled desires descended on me, implanting their talons ever deeper in my throbbing heart . . .

"One evening, a few months ago, we were once again in the library. It was already night, a clear summer night, and the moon trailed her long silver veil on the deserted sea. The moon silvered the thin stone mullions of the windows, the shimmering curtains, the black marble of the fireplace and a dark and infinitely deep mirror. It shone as well on the old gilded frames of pictures, the golden clovers of the ceiling, and the golden threads of the cornices. It danced upon glass doors, behind which books slumbered in heavy bindings and, without touching our couch, spread its pale sheet of light over the Persian rugs. To the right, the stained-glass in the casement window's head was obscure and in the background the lighted candelabra generated indecisive and multiple shadows that moved over the draperies in the light breeze.

"We were talking calmly, he sitting a little lower than I on cushions *she* had embroidered with royal crowns, me half-lying on the couch, my hand resting on his shoulder. Calmly, we were talking about her, as usual.

"'Oh yes,' said he, 'she was sweet, very sweet, in spite of her apparent pride. The words that escaped her lips were as sweet and tender as her melodious mouth, and she never uttered a hurtful word. Once—only once—her mouth darted a poisonous word . . .'

"'And what did she say, that one time?' I questioned.

"'I will avenge myself!'

"'But why? When?'

"'It was at the moment of her death . . .'

"'Her death?'

"Never before had he spoken of her death, as if he feared to envision its reality and disturb her beloved image with the horrible frights of decayed flesh.

"'Yes,' he continued, "she died when I stabbed her.'

"'Assassin!'

"I had exclaimed it in a whisper—and then we were as calm as before, as if nothing extraordinary had been said between us.

"'I stabbed her,' he said quietly, 'because she was certainly cheating on me. But then why, in dying, did she say, 'I will avenge myself!' and how did she hope to take revenge?'

"He was silent for a few moments, and without any impatience I waited for his story, *which I had always expected he would tell me.*

"'For months,' he continued at last, 'I knew that she was cheating on me—not in fact but in spirit alone, and no doubt that excused her in her own eyes, as if there is a difference between the sin lovingly dreamed of and the sin accomplished! I saw in her burning glances that she thought only of her desired lover.

92

"'I felt, at the feverish touch of her hand, at the sudden passion of her movements when drawing me to her, that she pictured another in my place. I loved her so much that, without worrying her with my clairvoyance and to save and preserve her, I had brought her here, far from the world, to this isolated dwelling. But it was too late, the evil was already irremediable. She no longer wished to fight against the adulterous thoughts which gave her pleasure, which she thought she could hide from me; no doubt judging them innocent as they could not be acted on without danger, since their object was far removed from her. I watched without her suspecting and, to prevent her suddenly leaving me if she was overcome by wickedness, I spread the rumor that her mind was disturbed. Also, confidants watched her comings and goings and, if she wanted to flee clandestinely, it would have been prevented. Did she nevertheless understand, despite precautions in my language and a constant and even temper, that I was suspicious, that I was *jealous*? Indeed, I sometimes caught in her eye a glimmer, not of suppressed love but of hatred, hatred against me . . . Oh, but her voice was so sweet, her grace so perfect, that only her eyes could betray her.

"'How was it so, and with what bitterness accumulated in my heart, that what eventually happened became possible?

"'That afternoon, specifically, no unhealthy thoughts affected my serenity—at my table I was writing and my left hand stroked Kadi's shimmering fur. The sun was about to set and, distracted, I looked up, to gaze at the golden globe that swung over the water . . .

"'At that moment a stifled sigh was heard behind me. I was not aware of Norah's presence, and her unexpected sigh surprised me. Without turning, I nervously grabbed a small sharp dagger that served as a letter opener . . . A second sigh was exhaled, weaker.

"'At this, I slowly turned my head. Mechanically clutching the handle of the dagger between my fingers, I looked at *her*. She was very pale, and tears were gathering at the edge of her eyelids. I mastered the sudden anger that ran through me from head to toe, because I believed that she was finally coming to confront me.

"'*Norah*, I asked jokingly. *Norah, were you looking for me?*

"'My look of attempted cheer provoked her own tender and pained countenance to suddenly harden, and she shrugged her shoulders.

"'I sat down beside her, and whispered in her ear: *Admit, admit that you do not want me, but instead you-know-who!*

"'An irresistible desire suddenly possessed me to extort the abominable confession.

"'She looked me in the face, singularly haughty and scornful, and without hesitation threw the deadly expected syllable straight into my heart:

"'*Yes!*

"'Quickly, my arm struck and I drove the small sharp blade deep into her throat.

"'*I will avenge myself!* she rasped.

"'I removed the dagger and dropped it to the ground. A stream of blood spurted from the wound and her eyes went out.

"'She had risen slightly as the blow struck her. Now, she was sitting as before, her head only a little tilted, and she seemed to be sleeping . . .'

"Emmanuel was silent.

"Without any terror, without any repulsion, I heard his story. I listened to it like a well-known childhood fable, sweetly repeated.

"'And blood flowed abundantly?' I ventured.

"'Did it flow? It spread out in a large puddle on the crimson carpet, to the very foot of this couch, during the day the violet light of the stained-glass windows made the blood appear violet as well, and then the night came and it looked black . . . But Kadi jumped to the ground, sniffed it, and dipped the tip of her tongue in, so I took away the resistant cat . . . and later, I returned to the room and discovered that Norah, the poor madwoman, had committed suicide . . .'

"A long silence rose again, a troubled silence of mute thoughts and memories . . .

"'And I never felt remorse,' he continued, 'never. Why should I, since she was guilty? Ah, but regrets, yes, I had bitter regrets because I loved her passionately. Regrets that have saturated my years with bitterness, and still I am intensely astonished at her incomprehensible final threat: *I will avenge myself!* What was the enigmatic sense of it? How would she revenge herself? Did she not understand that she was dying? Yet, with what little time she had left, she focused on this idea of certain revenge. Or did she believe that, troubled by my crime, my conscience would make my life intolerable? But my conscience never reproached me, and her spilled blood left no trace on my hands or in my mind.'

"His eyes were lost in shadows, and he paused. After an interval of silence he repeated:

"'Was it not strange, that vain menace from her moribund mouth: *I will avenge myself?*'

"I did not answer, but while I caressed his head, which rested on my breast, I thought of *her*, who I understood so well, who I had *almost already become*. And now she passed between us, looking into my eyes with a supplicating expression and said to me—I heard her distinctly: "Welcome me, welcome me!"

"I closed my eyes and for a moment, so short that *he* did not even notice, I was as dead. When I came back to myself, a little laugh shook me. 'I will avenge myself, I will avenge myself,' I chuckled . . .

"Emmanuel did not suspect that I was laughing, and thought only that I was trembling.

"'Are you afraid of me or her?' he asked, incredulously, for he knew that in everything I thought like him, and that I could only approve of him.

"For my answer, I kissed the hands that had killed . . .

"After that, I no longer needed to think of her. I thought *with her*, as she had entered me and her soul had become twin sister of my own, and I talked with her always, as she repeated, whether she wanted it or not: 'I will avenge myself, I will avenge myself . . .' These singular, terrible dialogues between our two souls . . . I vainly wished to remove myself from them. But my soul was too weak and was forced to yield to the *other's*, who detailed to it her ignored martyrdom's final, bloody scene, and assured my soul of her inevitable vengeance . . .

"And Emmanuel saw nothing, guessed nothing. He found me only ever more like Norah and, so, loved me more . . .

"But now, you will hear the end," she said panting, "because the sun is approaching the sea . . .

"Yesterday," she resumed, in a very low voice, as if we had shared some mysterious secret, "yesterday my soul slept deeply and the *other,* alone, watched inside of me. What she had done to lull my soul to sleep I do not know, but my body and mind did everything that *she,* the *other* one living there, desired. She handled them as she pleased, poured into my brain her most subtle thoughts, sped or slowed the beating of my heart, and directed all my movements as she liked.

"A little before sunset, Emmanuel entered the library. Automatically, with her steps, I went towards him. In my hand was a sharp little dagger, the very one with which he had killed her, and at the moment he sat on the divan I plunged it into his neck and removed it, shouting: 'My revenge!'

"A muffled cry came from his throat, and the *other* in me read with ferocious joy an unspeakable terror in the sudden enlargement of his pupils, for he had had time to recognize her.

"At that moment my soul woke up.

"I saw—without surprise, as one sees a familiar performance—I saw Emmanuel sinking on the cushions, and already he seemed to be sleeping. The blood ran down the red carpet, and I noticed with a smile that the violet light of the stained-glass turned the large pool of blood violet.

And mechanically I murmured: "Vengeance! Avenged!" obeying the *other*, who was still in me. As night fell, the puddle grew black, Kadi brushed against my unmoving form and, with shining eyes, dipped the tip of her tongue into the blood. Then I seized her in my arms and carried her off, though she struggled, and I lost consciousness..."

✳

She closed her eyes and in a voice growing ever softer, her hand pointed at the door on the right, she murmured:

"The sun sinks into the sea, and the *other* is there. Do you not see her? Look at her, but do not disturb her ... The light is purple near the open windows, the ray that falls through the windows is purple, and in that sinister purple beam she moves back and forth, looking for the red carpet that is there no more, and the smell of spilled blood intoxicates her ...

"The sun plunges under the ocean, the light falling from the stained-glass windows is gray. She pulls away, she seeks me, she is coming, she is coming!"

She sat up straight in bed, screaming and wringing her hands.

"Stop her from approaching, I do not want to ... I do not want to receive her any more! ... I'm afraid," she said in a guttural voice that chilled us ..."

Tears ran down her cheeks.

Suddenly, she clutched her chest with both hands, sank to the bed and said: "I will avenge myself!"

And as her expression suddenly grew calm, we did not immediately understand that she was dead, carrying the mysterious menace with her into eternity ...

THE ATONEMENT

"YOU say that there is no immanent justice and that no one is so avenged for the harm done to him by others as when he takes vengeance himself? What do you know? First of all, in many cases it is materially impossible for us to reach the person who injured us, whether the action was surreptitious and hidden or the secret was only revealed after their death. Yet Destiny can, without our knowing it, extend its hand and inflict upon them a punishment which exceeds our most ferocious wishes."

Until now, Roger Valtet had listened to our discussion without participating in it, according to his habit. Here he intervened with a surprising vehemence. For the sake of his great age, we refrained from contradicting him. But Roger Valtet continued, spontaneously:

"Are you incredulous? You demand proof: and then, what does it even matter to us if Fate strikes, if we do not know? It's because we do not always know it; it sometimes manifests its occult power in a dreadful way. In support, do you want me to tell you a story that is personal to me, and about which I have always remained silent? Now that years have elapsed, I can speak of it, without fearing that the wound of a healed heart will be reopened.

"You believe me to be an unrepentant celibate. Yet I was married. I was no longer young when I married, out of love, a foreigner who brought me nothing but marvelous beauty. I had a small pension, a situation, a red ribbon; I was without family. It seemed to me that a legitimate companion would ennoble my life. In truth, I did not think about it until after meeting, in a friend's salon, a relative of the masters of the house, newly arrived from Australia. I was told she was an orphan, very poor and in search of gainful employment. I was indignant that such a pretty girl needed to work to live, as she had been made to receive homage and dictate her caprices, and I dared tell her this. Her smile was delicious and sad; the charm of her naïve answer was increased by her exotic accent. I frequented my friends more often than usual, and they realized before I did that I was in love with Miss Jane, and worked behind the scenes. Through their care, we were betrothed, though I did not think myself worthy of Jane. I was more a slave than a husband, but so sweet was slavery!

"Jane loved luxury, and my modest income could not meet her needs. I struggled to satisfy her, and discovered in my mind new resources for gold. For the cost of excessive labor, I realized some notable profits; and so she had the *toilettes* that suited her and an elegant living environment that harmonized with her beauty. She rewarded me with kisses and cuddles. I applied my strength to dogged work. The mirror showed me a tired, prematurely faded image of myself. At my side, Jane was the perfect creature, the young sultaness whom I dreamed of in my adolescence. I told her so, and also told her that I was ugly and old and begged pardon for associating her youthful grace with my senility. Speaking in this way I exaggerated, but she shut my mouth with her little hand, laughingly kissed my eyes, and said: 'You are young and handsome, since you are intelligent and I love you.' And I believed her. I had absolute confidence in her; her gaze was limpid and frank. I felt this so completely that never did the slightest suspicion of her touch me. I did not even think of being jealous. Sometimes, however, she would be strangely removed. If I questioned her, she apologized for reflecting on her childhood and distant homeland. And I still believed her. To distract her, I took her to the theater. I do not know what pleased her the most, to see what was happening on the stage, or to be seen herself and admired by the spectators. It was the opportunity for her to show her jewels, for which she had a passion.

"Jewelry! I had bought her a lot and had spent a small fortune to establish her jewelry box. But she always needed new designs, and she would beg me so sweetly that I managed to satisfy her. Once, however, I had to refuse her. A necklace in the window of a jeweler, formed of a lace of fine gold and adorned with a precious enchained ring, had seduced her. With the tip of her little finger, she pointed to it: 'I would like this necklace,' she told me. I reasoned with her. My cash flow was greatly reduced, I had payments to make. She agreed to wait for a more opportune moment. 'But, then,' she said, 'the necklace will be sold!' I held my ground. She sulked at me. In the evening, she whispered in my ear: 'It was a desire that has already passed out of me!'

"Knowing she was pregnant filled me with joy. I would have liked to have run to the jeweler's, and bring her the desired object. Then I thought that money would be needed in the household. And besides, she had already just confessed to me that she did not care any more about the necklace. But that same night, Jane felt very ill. I had to go and get a doctor.

"I will not describe the phases of the sickness, which was quickly fatal. In the delirium of agony, Jane often repeated: 'The necklace, the necklace!' I reproached myself bitterly for not having been able to obey her last desire, and just before the final moment I put the golden chain in her hands, and then placed it around her neck. Her fingers felt it, closed around it. It seemed to me that she was smiling. 'You'll heal,' I whispered. But she did not hear me anymore: she had just expired. The enchained ring sparkled on her chest.

"It is useless for me to tell you what my despair was like. I wanted Jane to be buried with the necklace, the last adornment I had been able to offer her, and my only remorse.

"Her body, which rested on a padded bier, was provisionally deposited in a suburban graveyard, while waiting to be transported to its final resting place in my native town, where I had acquired a plot for Jane and myself. I had a vault carefully built, and a monument that perpetuated my grief.

"Months passed. I spent days in Jane's room, surrounded by memories of her, talking to her ghost. Sometimes I opened the jewelry box. Like so many beloved eyes, jewels considered me with their varied facets. And then a hidden spring gave way under the involuntary push of my finger. In a small secret drawer was a tight little wad of papers. I drew it into the light: letters and telegrams scattered. The writings were diverse; no signatures, or simple initials. But the text was uniform, declarations, rendezvous, offers of money or gifts . . . Jane, the candid, the delicious Jane had cheated on me in the most odious and disgusting way . . . I remember that I cried all that night, shaking with anger and hatred. I wanted to kill, but who? I cursed Destiny and my own helplessness. Then I burned all the anonymous papers. I sold the jewels, I left the apartment where I had lived with Jane, and I mourned my atrocious sorrow in silence, in stupidity, in forgetfulness. Yes, I thought, I could forget. At its height, pain becomes indifference.

"But, the legal span of time having passed, I was warned that the temporary grave concession was over. I had to oversee the transfer of Jane's body to the place I had chosen. I had to be present at the exhumation. I fulfilled my duty.

"When we opened the coffin, I turned my eyes away. 'Lies and rot,' I told myself. 'Jane was only a lie, and now I do not want to know what has become of her flesh . . . 'In spite of myself, my eyelids swelled with tears and I do not know what strange and sweet vertigo drew me towards the gaping pit.

"A cry filled me with terror.

"'Horrible!' said one of the assistants.

"In my turn I leaned over the bier. And then, I saw . . . O the abominable vision . . . I stared, as if I did not discern anything, then I fell on my knees, stammering (and, God forgive me, laughing, but I had gone crazy!): 'the beggar, she has done herself justice!' Then I lost consciousness. I woke up in a hospital ward.

"What did I see? The gold lace was twisted around Jane's wrists. Her outstretched arms had tightened with all their might, the ring was embedded in the vertebrae of her neck. Jane, buried alive, had strangled herself with the necklace, my last present . . .

"Did not Destiny really take my revenge? Too much, even! I would have been less cruel. So I forgave Jane. And if I have wronged someone, I pray God will forgive me . . ."

And Roger Valtet fell into a gloomy silence.

THE STRANGER

WE went up the Champs-Elysees where the carriages continued to flow, although they grew rarer by the minute, while the slowly setting July sun enveloped the Arc de Triomphe in an august purple. Flowers of bloody silk and magnificent gold dust glorified the entire length of the Triumphal Avenue. Less attentive to the perfection of the scene than to the comings and goings of the crowd, my countryman Maurice Sayan, a poet more rich in money than rhymes and a notorious lover, was communicating to me his opinion on the aesthetics of the summer fashions, when a victoria came to pass very close to us at a slow pace. A single woman was enthroned therein; her priestly attitude and the Junoesque beauty of her body, which flourished in the finery of an exquisite sumptuousness, made me want to see her face, entirely hidden by a thick veil. Maurice Sayan made a gesture of surprise:

"It is her!" he exclaimed.

The stranger turned, the gleam of her gaze drifting to him. Immediately she leaned towards the coachman, gave an order, the horses reared up and the carriage sped away quickly, disappearing in a cloud of dust before Maurice had recovered from his astonishment.

"Who was *she*?" I asked.

"Ah! Yes, you do not know. It's a story I kept quiet about. Besides, I do not know exactly who *she* is, although I have seen her closely—I mean very closely. Let's walk, and I'll tell you.

"It was in this very same season, on the shores of Lake Como in Bellagio. Tourists hardly frequent there, stopping there even less during the summer, under the vain pretext that it suffers from the heat. This is fortunate, for they abandon to the dreamers the solitary splendor of its enchanting banks, where rich blossoms exhale eloquent, sensual perfumes for the pleasure of the privileged. The deserted marble villas are beautiful in their cypress settings. The water spreads from one dark promontory to the other in an intense purple and the sharp peaks tear at the deep azure of the sky if they are not buried in the heavy clouds where storms accumulate, threatening to transfigure the countryside with the wildness of lightning.

"From the hotel where I stayed, I selfishly enjoyed the landscape, renewed under such varied lighting conditions. I also enjoyed the singularly captivating sight of a young woman, the only traveler who lingered in the place. In the evening, on the neighboring balcony, she leaned over and, with a long look, embraced the expanse of the water where the scalloped mountains were inverted. I loved her romantic pose. She had long white fingers adorned with jewels, which I longed to see stroking the strings of a harp. Her profile, haloed by blonde hair of extreme delicacy, stood out against the green background of the sky as pure as a cameo, disdainful and sad. Although she dressed with a luxury of rather bad taste, either as a showy princess or a *demi-mondaine*, her light silks showed the sculptural lines of her body, and old but priceless lace highlighted the delicacy of her wrists and the fullness of her chest.

"Princess or *demi-mondaine*? At the hotel she was treated as a princess, for her haughty and silent manner commanded respect; and, moreover, she paid extravagantly. Who she was we did not know. She had registered under a name evidently borrowed, so common it was, and her chambermaid had the noble airs of a lady of honor. According to her name and because of her manners, the staff simply called her: Her Highness Nathalie.

"A little mystery is enough to awaken the curiosity of an idle poet. Around Her Highness Nathalie I imagined a lot of mystery, while thinking it a good idea to fall madly in love with her. All that was unknown about her pleased me. She seduced me, appearing alone in the amethyst evenings, bending over the melodious lake that vibrated from her nostalgic thought, while the curve of her body revealed some adorable secrets which moved me. The rose beds in the gardens and the magnolias carried white flowers with contours less pure than her divine breasts beneath the fabric of her transparent bodice. One night, on the clear screen of her curtain, I saw her naked shadow . . . I loved Nathalie from then on, and desired to substitute a buxom reality for that magic shadow.

"Meeting her was not easy. She left infrequently, and at irregular hours, to take her boat, in which her royal stature was sheltered under a canopy. The vigorous oars drove her away from the shore, an impassive idol decreasing in the field of my binoculars.

"Seizing the right moment more than once, under any pretext, I tried to approach her. With a gesture, or a short word, she acknowledged and dismissed me. I persisted, and so I learned one morning that Her Highness Nathalie had decided to leave Bellagio and was on her way to an unknown destination. The news irritated me and I called myself a fool, a ridiculous novice, inventing after the fact a whole system of irresistible seductions. I took care to track the fugitive, but there was no trace: Nathalie had escaped from the line of my horizon and, for a long time, she was for me only a memory, an image of mystery and beauty that I liked to evoke in a shimmer of silky water and velvet greenery, at dusk among perfumes.

"But I found her, in the most unexpected and simple way, in Paris itself. Last year, at the beginning of the autumn, I was walking not far from home, in the alleys of La Muette. A warm, humid wind lifted the dead leaves, and amused me with their complicated and fantastic play as twilight invaded the park. Following the whirlwinds, I was led to the gate of a villa at the moment when the door opened, giving passage to a woman of majestic appearance, in whom I immediately recognized my stranger. She too recognized me, because I could not restrain myself from uttering aloud: 'Nathalie!' And, after withdrawing in surprise and then changing her mind, she came straight to me, with an angry look and shouted:

"'What do you want of me? Who are you? A spy?'

"'An amorous man,' I stammered without acknowledging the insult, whose meaning I didn't understand.

"She shrugged. 'A madman then,' she said. 'Were you the one in Bellagio, following me constantly?'

"'Ah, do you remember? From the first I admired you and loved you.'

"'Thank you for saying it. This moment is well chosen. Goodbye, sir. We will not see each other again, I hope.'

"And, closing the door suddenly, she returned to the villa.

"For me, less disconcerted by the lack of welcome than I was happy from the encounter, that evening I wrote a daring and naïve epistle that I slipped into the mailbox of the gate and the following day I presented myself at the villa.

"'Pooh!' I said to encourage myself, 'a *demi-mondaine* who makes me posture. We'll see . . .'

"And my heart beat hard when, having handed over my card, instead of being rejected, the valet introduced me into a spacious living room where, as if she was giving me an audience or preparing to pay an invoice, Nathalie received me. She held my letter in her hand.

"'What is this joke?' she asked sternly. 'Take back this paper. No one writes love letters to me.'

"Her long silk skirt unfurled behind her as, raising her waist, her imperious head tilted to one side.

"Troubled, intimidated, I was looking for the right reply. I chose, among others, a stupid phrase from a novel that I articulated with sincerity:

"'You see in front of you, madam, a man who is going to kill himself, if . . .'

"'If what?' she interrupted. 'What can it mean to me that you kill yourself? You will have just wasted time since Bellagio.'

"Suddenly, her eyes softened and her tone died down:

"'Do you know why I first fled you, and why now I have received you, and you alone, after having lived in perfect solitude for years?' she asked. 'It is because you resemble someone, and the more I consider you, the more this resemblance asserts itself. It makes me suffer, and my eyes feed on it. Sit. I know, because I looked into it, that you are a gallant man. I will not confide in you, but in speaking to you it seems to me that I speak with a resuscitated dead man. Listen to me.'

"She gradually exalted: 'I am a dead woman, dead to the world, which must not know that I exist. Ah! If you knew the drama . . . if I dared, if I were allowed to express myself! The stone of an implacable silence weighs on my heart, as on a tomb where a tragic secret sleeps. I preserve myself, a widow without having been a wife, intact for an august memory. Ah, how you look like him!'

"'She is mad,' I said to myself, without attaching much meaning to her words, 'but how beautiful she is! Her eyes are as green as the emerald on her ring finger.'

"And leaving her to talk, I got drunk on her voice, and suffered the dizzying appeal of her eyes, the rhythm of her body. It seemed to me that my destiny was bound.

"'Come,' she said, 'it will be evening soon, and it is the hour when sadness rises everywhere. I love to rock along with the slow trot of horses. This single, unique time you will accompany me. By my side, you will be the illusion, the incarnate ghost of the person I cherished.'

"So, under the foliage of pale gold and faded purple, the victoria rolled gently in the wood, which was being depopulated as the night invaded it. And Nathalie started again.

"'Ah! If you only knew who I am! For all, I am dead, and for him alone, my royal lover who perished . . . ah! . . . in what bloody drama, I still live. And until my last breath I would like to remain beautiful for him!'

"Slowly, I pulled her against me, her waist folded in my arms, my mouth searched for her mouth.

"'Ah, this is wrong!' she moaned. 'He will take revenge. You are the devil and, to defeat me, you have stolen the likeness of another!'

"But she abandoned herself and so much did I desire her that I took no pity on her for being mad.

"A hard shock threw us apart. How the accident happened, I do not know. Our coachman, no doubt sleepy, heard the alarm call too late and at the turn of the road the carriage toppled over.

"I got up quickly, having no trouble, only a little stunned. But Nathalie . . . she had been thrown on the sidewalk, face forward. She was screaming; blood was streaming down her face, so marvelous the moment before, and now disfigured, frightful . . . I closed my eyes and a vision interposed, that of the bloody and disfigured corpse of the royal lover, whom she had spoken of to me without naming . . .

"I fled through the woods. I have not seen Mathilde[1] since then and now we have met suddenly, so that I must tell you of my adventure. You understand now why this stranger hid her face under an impenetrable veil.

"But," I asked after a moment's thought, "do you really think that Nathalie is the officially dead but actually living heroine in a historical and princely drama?"

"I want to believe it," Sayan replied. "Only stories we believe in are true."

---

1 The name Mathilde is in the original text and might or might not be an error.

A PARTIAL LIST OF SNUGGLY BOOKS